27 VIEWS OF CHAPEL HILL

A Real nice Place to Live

CROOK'S CORNER
GOOD FOOD

SINCE 1922!
CAROLINA COFFEE

OLD intimate Book-SHOP
FAULKNER was HERE!

THIS IS A BASKETBALL

DRUGSTORE + Soda fountain
SUTTON'S
SINCE 1923!

UNC

James TAYLOR

Post OFFICE COURT HOUSE
BUILT in 1937!

MOREHEAD PLANETARIUM

FRANKLIN Street

27 VIEWS OF CHAPEL HILL

A Southern University Town in Prose & Poetry

Introduction by Daniel Wallace

eno
publishers

27 Views of Chapel Hill: A Southern University Town in Prose & Poetry
Introduction by Daniel Wallace
© Eno Publishers, 2011

Each selection is the copyrighted property of its respective author
or publisher, if so noted on Permissions page, and appears in this volume
by arrangement with the individual writer or publisher.

Eno Publishers
P.O. Box 158
Hillsborough, North Carolina 27278
www.enopublishers.org

ISBN-13: 978-0-9820771-9-1
ISBN-10: 0-982-0771-9-x
Library of Congress Control Number: 2011927629
Printed in the United States
10 9 8 7 6 5 4 3 2 1

Cover illustration by Daniel Wallace, Chapel Hill, North Carolina
Design and typesetting by Horse & Buggy Press, Durham, North Carolina
Distributed to the book trade by John F. Blair Publisher, 800.222.9796

Acknowledgments

Eno Publishers wishes to acknowledge the generous support of the Orange County Arts Commission in helping to fund the editorial and production costs of 27 *Views of Chapel Hill.*

The publisher also wishes to thank Gita Schonfeld, Katie Saintsing, and Speed Hallman for their careful reading of the views, and Daniel Wallace — writer, artist, friend — for his colorful rendering of Franklin Street.

A huge thank you to our twenty-nine writers (twenty-seven, plus two) who have created a literary snapshot of Chapel Hill, now and then.

Permissions

Some of the works in this volume have appeared in whole or in part in other publications.

A version of David E. Brown's "Chapel Hill: The War Years" originally appeared in the *Carolina Alumni Review* (September 1995).

A version of Nic Brown's "A Love Letter" was first published in the *Chapel Hill News* (2 June 2010).

A portion of the introduction from Mildred Council's cookbook, *Mama Dip's Kitchen* (1999, University of North Carolina Press), appears here courtesy of the publisher.

A version of "The Sisters' Garden," by D.G. Martin, appeared in *Our State Magazine* (April 2005).

A version of Michael McFee's *"Fragrantissima"* originally appeared in the *Carolina Alumni Review* (January/February 1997).

A version of "Where the Parking Lot Is Now," by Sy Safransky, was originally published in the *Sun* (April 1996).

Jim Seay's "Down among the Bones, the Darks, the Sparrows" was first published in the *Independent Weekly*, www.indyweek.com (10 November 2010).

A version of "Muslims in the Cul-de-sac," by Samia Serageldin, originally appeared in *Love Is Like Water and Other Stories*, published by Syracuse University Press (2009), and appears here courtesy of the publisher.

A version of Bland Simpson's "In Battle's Park" originally appeared in *Wildlife in North Carolina* (February 1995).

Elizabeth Spencer's "Rising Tide" originally appeared in the *Oxford American*, Spring 2010.

A version of Wells Towers's essay, "Life on the Hill," previously appeared in *Garden & Gun* (August 2009).

Daphne Athas's "The Library" is excerpted from *Entering Ephesus*, reissued by Second Chance Press (1991).

Will Blythe's "The Religion of the Forehead" is excerpted from *To Hate Like This Is to Be Happy Forever*, published by itbooks (2006), a division of HarperCollins Publishers.

Table of Contents

🦎 FANS & FRIENDS

🦎 FRIENDS & NEIGHBORS

STREET SCENES

A PLACE APART

VIEWS FROM BEFORE

VIEWS IN FICTION

IN THE REARVIEW MIRROR

Preface

27 VIEWS OF CHAPEL HILL is just that: twenty-seven different stories and poems that capture some aspect of life in the eponymous southern university town that many writers call home. Although this book turns out to include twenty-nine views, not just twenty-seven, it barely scrapes Chapel Hill's broad literary surface. But it's a start.

In some of the views, Chapel Hill is front and center; in others the town provides a backdrop. Some celebrate the town; others expose its complicated past and even more complicated present, its struggles with inequality, authenticity, growth, cultural change. Still others tell of personal connections to place and to one another. This collection offers a diversity of generations, ethnicity, life experiences, genres—fiction, essays, poems, even a letter written to the entire town.

Our hope is that this small chorus of voices creates a sort of genius loci, giving readers insight into who we are and who we were, how we think about where we live, how we see ourselves. Perhaps it also will inspire us to reflect on how the community informs the arts, and vice versa.

Most of all we hope all twenty-nine of our *27 Views of Chapel Hill* provide a sense of place, the spirit of place.

Elizabeth Woodman
Eno Publishers | Summer 2011

Introduction

IN THE BEGINNING, before there was anybody here at all—before Chapel Hill, before Carrboro, even before Historic Hillsborough; before Franklin Street, skinny lattes, even before Dean Smith—this postage stamp of soil we now occupy was just an undefined mass of pine trees, parakeets, possums, and dirt. It was not *known* for anything; it was not *famous* for anything; it was not *named* anything. People came here because they were on their way somewhere else, and this happened to be the place where their horse died and it was easier just to settle down than it was to get another horse. And that, in a nutshell, is how Chapel Hill came to be.[1]

But over time everywhere gets to be known as *something*. Beaver, Oklahoma, for instance, is known as the Cow Chip Throwing Capital of the World. The Bratwurst Capital of the World is, of course, Sheboygan, Wisconsin.[2] And though Chapel Hill is not officially the capital of the world of anything, it has, over the years, become the home of more writers than any other single town in the world.[3] They come here— novelists, poets, writers of nonfiction and historical fiction, of Southern

---

1 This is, of course, pure conjecture. Absolutely no research has been performed to determine the accuracy of this statement, and none ever will be, by this writer.

2 The list goes on. The Red Flannel Capital of the World is Cedar Springs, Michigan; the Sock Capital of the World is Fort Payne, Alabama. Et cetera. To list them here in their entirety would take minutes, perhaps an entire hour.

3 This is not a fact, inasmuch as it has been proven, tested, or studied. But I'm not aware of any other town, except Historic Hillsborough, that makes this claim, and we might as well be almost the first.

fiction and Northern fiction, television writers, movie writers, and radio commentators, writers of history, scholarly tracts, James Bond thrillers, all kinds of writers, dead and living alike. Even the guy who writes the ingredients label on the side of cereal boxes — *he* lives here.[4]

Some Chapel Hill writers toil in near-anonymity. Many, though, are exceptionally famous, and to mention them by name would be no more than a chest-thumping braggadocio. What the hell. Let's chest-thump: Just turn back to the Table of Contents of 27 *Views of Chapel Hill.* And names aren't important anyway: Everybody knows this ground is fertile with ink-stained wretches of every stripe.[5]

The question is *why?* Why here and not there? What is so great about Chapel Hill that writers want to live here, in such numbers that it has been said by swinging a dead cat (don't try this at home), you are likely to hit or offend one, or at least get written about by one of them as the crazy guy who swung a dead cat that day?

Why did they come, these writers, and why did they stay?

Here is my theory: Thomas Wolfe and William Faulkner. They're the reason. Thomas Wolfe was born in Asheville, and he attended the University of North Carolina at Chapel Hill, matriculating when he was *fifteen years old.* William Faulkner wasn't born here, and he didn't go to school at Carolina. As a young man though he *came* here. He visited. Apparently he was drunk every second. It's reported that he even lost a page of the manuscript he was working on — *Light in August.* But sober or not, he was here. Much later, Faulkner said Wolfe was his generation's best writer — listing himself as second, which is a *kind* of humility, I guess. It also may well be true.[6] They are, indisputably, among the greatest of American writers.

Carrying my theory through to its logical conclusion, the presence of Faulkner and Wolfe in Chapel Hill caused something to happen:

---

4 Also not a proven fact.

5 What does that mean, "every stripe"? I have no idea.

6 I don't really know.

germination. There's a picture of Faulkner at the old Intimate Bookshop, sadly no longer extant, a place Wolfe doubtlessly visited himself, post-graduation. The magic of their talent was so prodigious and original, so *fecund* (a word both were known to use on occasion) that as each passed through the same place—maybe walking past shelves stocked with Fiction: Southern, where maybe they sat *in the same chair*—something amazing formed. A seed was planted and a flower grew, and it's this flower—the scent of which is irresistible to any writer worth his or her salt—that draws so many of us to Chapel Hill.

And here we are—ninety years after Wolfe graduated from UNC, seventy years since Faulkner strolled down Franklin Street—a town full of writers, a town full of stories. *27 Views of Chapel Hill* offers up some of that prose and poetry. It doesn't even try to be comprehensive, which is really a testament to this—yes—*fecund* environment. So many wonderful writers live here, it's impossible to fit them all in one volume. To do that, Eno Publishers would have had to change the title to *27,000 Views of Chapel Hill.* Because everybody has their own view, every writer, every reader. Here are a few of them. Enjoy.

Daniel Wallace
Summer 2011

DANIEL WALLACE is a Chapel Hill writer and illustrator. He has written five novels, including *Big Fish* and, most recently, *Mr. Sebastian and the Negro Magician.* He writes a monthly humor column in *Our State Magazine.* He is director of the Creative Writing Program at the University of North Carolina at Chapel Hill. His illustration of Franklin Street appears on the cover of *27 Views of Chapel Hill.*

Fans & Friends

Life on the Hill

WELLS TOWER

CHAPEL HILL IS A TOWN I wish I loved less than I do. I have lived in Louisiana, New Zealand, Oregon, Canada, Connecticut, Scotland, and New York City (where I presently dwell), yet I have never been entirely happy in any of these places, because, like the fool who can't rid his head of memories of the girl he adored in eighth grade, I cannot let go of my hometown.

Sometimes described by its boosters as "the pat of butter in a sea of grits," Chapel Hill (and its adjunct community, Carrboro) lies on a belt of high and wooded ground two and half hours from the Atlantic Ocean and three east of the Appalachian range. We are 140 miles east of Charlotte, and twenty-five minutes north of Raleigh, our capital. But Chapel Hill's citizens understand that what makes our town so agreeable is not that it lies in the gravitational field of other destinations, but that it is politely and resolutely a distinct place with an array of magnetisms (often counter-poised) entirely its own.

Chapel Hill's Southernness is fitful. Our cosmopolitan vanity is wounded when friends in New York or Los Angeles say insufferable things like "Well, it all sounds very nice, but I could never live in the *South*." We retort heatedly with examples of our village's urbanity: its art house movie theaters (we have two!), our socialist bookshop (it occupies the lower floor of a venerable massage parlor), and the roster of dining establishments of which the James Beard Foundation has taken notice. Or we mention that, thanks to the University of North Carolina (America's first public university), Chapel Hill has the highest concentration of PhDs in the United States. They have fetched up and washed out here in such numbers that you can hardly get your oil changed without the Jiffy Lube attendant offering his maunderings on Kierkegaard. We talk about the magicians of science out in the Research Triangle Park, designing snazzy new antibiotics and long polymers. We mention our cherished nightclub, Cat's Cradle, and our indie music boom in the 1990s, when bands like Superchunk, Polvo, and the Squirrel Nut Zippers convinced hundreds of young hairy people to load their cars with guitars and amplifiers and drive to our town. Or we quote the late, long-reigning right-wing troglodyte Senator Jesse Helms, who, when asked his opinion about construction of a new state zoo, said, disdaining our un-Dixielike political tendencies, "Why do we need a zoo when we could just put up a fence around Chapel Hill?"

And yet: while Red State Carolina may scoff at Chapel Hill and Carrboro's dubious Southern bona fides, I submit that we have salvaged most of what is good about the Southern way of things and left the unpleasant bits at the curb. Our schools are excellent, and yoga is a local epidemic, yet on a summer night in Carrboro, you need not look far to find porches stocked with people plucking banjos with utmost sincerity. In our downtown, million-dollar green-built condominiums are springing up like kudzu shoots, but we still have springtime eruptions of old-growth azalea and dogwood blossoms to gobsmack a Savannahian. Free parking is increasingly hard to come by, but drive three miles to the north or west, and you are in swaying cornscapes and pasturelands comely enough to stop your heart. We have three "progressive" grocery stores and uncountable espresso peddlers, yet we are, to a citizen, people who will clench fists

24

and go red in the face if told there are ways to eat pulled pork other than in a rinse of vinegar and pepper flakes.

Even as sprawl metastasizes at our margins and Priuses eclipse Ford pickups in the vehicle registry, we are a people nearly wretched with nostalgia. "How many Chapel Hillians does it take to change a light bulb?" runs an old joke. "Ten: one to change it and nine to moon about how great the old light bulb was." The antique rites of village life are important to us. To pass an acquaintance on the sidewalk without saying anything is to gravely breach the social code (you're acquainted with the entire phone book if you've been here more than two years). Urban transplants scorn our sociability as fraudulent Mayberryism, but we understand that the health of a community sometimes depends on listening to news that you are not interested in while the milk goes warm in your grocery bag. Sentimental bootleggers still sell moonshine in the outer county. Whole-hog cookery remains a cherished rite, and you cannot ascend to plenary status as a Chapel Hill native if you have not thrown at least one pig-picking.

Not long ago, I roasted my first hog with my friend Matt Neal, son of the great, departed chef Bill Neal, whose restaurant Crook's Corner reintroduced shrimp and grits to the world. It was a chilly evening, and we stayed up all night, drinking bourbon, shoveling applewood embers into the cooker's belly. We dared not open the cooker's top, for fear we'd lose precious warmth and sour the meat. When we lifted the lid the following morning, we were surprised to find that the pig was on fire and had been that way for eight hours at least. We hosed it off. It looked like a fallen meteorite, but dressed out at eighty pounds of good flesh. These days, Matt operates, contrarily, Neal's Deli, a New York–style deli in Carrboro. His sandwiches surpass any I've found in my Brooklyn neighborhood. He does not sell barbecue.

Many of our citizens would tell you that the town's most essential tribal marrow lies in our hatred of the sports teams and athletics fans of Duke University in Durham. ("Hatred" is not too strong a word. Multiple books have been written about the purity of our loathing.) However, I think we privately adore Duke. Duke, which is exclusive, and expensive, and chiefly attended by people from New Jersey, allows us to feel like up-from-the-red-clay salt-of-the-earthers when we root for UNC, which is also exclusive, but a good value for its tuition, and which admits at least a token quota of North Carolinians. We might think the emerald quads and oak-limb vaultings of the UNC campus a bit too glorious and prepossessing if it weren't for Duke's architecture, built, supposedly, to replicate Princeton when Princeton could not be bribed into renaming itself "Duke." The result is a gaudy fantasyland of leaded glass and Gothic spires raised in vulgar inversion of our state's fine motto, *Esse quam videri*: "To be, rather than to seem."

To my mind, Chapel Hill's highest virtue is not its brittle preoccupations with sports or provincial tradition but the limberness of the place. It is a Shangri-la of indeterminacy: neither fusty Old South sanctum nor soulless New South suburb, neither metropolis nor boondocks. To live easefully in New York or New Orleans, one must strive to be a New Yorker or a New Orleanian. In Chapel Hill, a town too genial to demand much of its people, one can simply be.

In Chapel Hill, life is at once simple and civilized. I look forward to one day moving home to a town where basketball season and tomato season at the farmer's market arrive to nearly equal fanfare, a pony-size city where you can catch a performance by a superb garage band or a world-class orchestra without worrying that your car is being stripped in the parking lot, a place to wake on weekend mornings to the sound of a police siren that on second hearing turns out to be a mourning dove moaning in the pines.

WELLS TOWER is the author of *Everything Ravaged, Everything Burned* and many short stories. His feature articles have appeared in numerous publications, including *Harper's* and *GQ*. He was named one of the *New Yorker's* "20 Under 40," the nation's luminary fiction writers under forty years old.

Sweeter Still at Twelve

JOCK LAUTERER

I WASN'T ABLE TO ATTEND the gala at Memorial Hall a few years ago when UNC awarded James Taylor, my childhood chum, with a lifetime achievement award.

But even if I had been there and he had seen me, I'm certain JT wouldn't recognize his old guitar bud. See, both James and I have changed a wee bit since the late Fifties when we were twelve and fourteen, respectively. His hairline has receded and I've had a major recession.

But when we were kids, we were spend-the-night type of friends. On warm autumn evenings when I'd be invited to sleep over, we'd go to bed with the windows open, listening to the distant frat party music wafting from campus, the smooth black combos crooning "Handy Man," "Up on the Roof," and "How Sweet It Is to Be Loved by You."

James lived with brother Alex in what I considered to be Boy's Heaven: a modern, A-frame building with lots of glass and wood, actually separate from the family's contemporary-style main house in the Morgan Creek neighborhood.

James was an intense, thoughtful kid who didn't say a lot but whose dry sense of humor mirrored that of his eclectic family. In those days James was not so much into guitar as he was cello, though he took lessons in both. (I remember a polished honey-wooded cello sitting grandly in his room.) When I mentioned that my mother had an old guitar, James, in his typically generous fashion, offered to teach me.

It happened one bright January morning after I had spent the night at James's and a two-inch snowfall had forced the schools to close. But instead of the normal high spirits that accompanied a snow day, I became increasingly nervous as we tromped across town.

That James couldn't spend the night at my house was a great source of shame for me—and the very act of letting him into the house represented the sharing of a dark secret, cementing our bond. For nobody was allowed in our house. Nobody.

While bike riding three years prior, my older brother, Nick, had been struck and killed by a drunk driver. My mother, convinced that Nick was running away from home, blamed herself for his death, and dealt with the self-condemnation in her own way. From the day Nick died, she never touched the house again, except to put something down.

Thus, over the years, the rooms piled high with the detritus of guilt: old clothes, newspapers, books, *Life* magazines, layers of dust, unopened junk mail, papers—the effluvia of daily living covering, disguising, and burying any trace of my brother's presence. Windows became opaque with dust; trails between mounds of newspapers led from room to room; chairs became indistinguishable blobs of old stuff, stratified according to whenever Mom threw something down, where it lay until it, too, was covered by the next thing.

Into this forbidden Dickensian warehouse of a home, I admitted my buddy James.

He seemed not to notice the chaos, but went straight to the old 1930s guitar I dug out of a murky corner of the living room that doubled as my mom's bedroom. Sitting on my mother's unmade bed, he tuned the old guitar, his long, supple musician's fingers guiding me through G, C, and D7, my first chords played there in that dark childhood house of shame.

It's been over fifty years since that bright January day when James Taylor taught me to play the guitar. I lost touch with him the next year when his family sent him to private school. Since then, I've entertained the fantasy of reconnecting with JT, but always lose the nerve to make that phone call.

Still I have this wild fantasy that James will read this piece and phone me up: "Hey Jock, remember me? It's James—James Taylor. . . ."

Yeah right, and Roy Williams has just recruited me to play for the Heels. But James, if you do get this: "You've Got a Friend."

JOCK LAUTERER teaches at the School of Journalism and Mass Communication at the University of North Carolina at Chapel Hill. He is the author of six books, including *Wouldn't Take Nothin' for My Journey Now* and *Runnin' on Rims*. He is a monthly columnist for the *Carrboro Citizen*.

There Is a Light That Never Goes Out

LINNIE GREENE

WE DID IT EVERY WEEKEND. Piling into the black jeep—mix CDs stacked high on the dashboard—the four of us would roll the windows down and yell our favorite songs out of tune. By that point, we'd exhausted most options that were suitable for a bunch of high school seniors on a Saturday night. We had already tried the hookah bar, which made our voices sound more sickly than sexy. We had stolen beers and swigged them in the tree house, until our parents discovered that their supply was dwindling. We had come up with plenty of unsuccessful schemes. The Nightlight was a last-ditch effort: open to all ages, low door charge, low expectations.

Most of the time, we didn't know any of the bands that played there. A few hours before, there'd be a cursory search on MySpace, and even if the headliner described itself as "new-wave doom proto-metal with a Neil Diamond influence," we'd usually go anyway. We were not the kind of kids who got invited to parties, and on the rare occasions that we were, we still couldn't find anybody to buy us a case of beer. So there we were—driving down Highway 54 to the Nightlight, digging five bucks out of our pockets and hoping that we wouldn't feel quite so out of place.

It's a peculiar thing to discover a scene for the first time, and I can't say it was love at first sight. I felt awkward, too unhip to hang with the shaggy-haired musicians manning the bar and the waif-like girls wearing thrift store clothes. The only shows I'd caught at Cat's Cradle were the ones I saw with friends from school—young hot things with John Mayer vocals and minimal talent, the kind of shows marketed to high school girls and no one else.

The Nightlight was smaller, weirder—at that point, there were still a few bins of books in the corners and paintings hanging on the walls that looked like some anarchist had tried his hand at folk art. I was as intrigued by the place as I was by the music; the low-ceilinged space with no stage felt like I'd intruded into an artist's bedroom or an opium den. Sitting on a vinyl sofa between my three best friends, I felt like a fly on the wall, uninvited but unable to stop staring.

The show that still sticks in my memory is a set from Run Dan Run, a pop and electronic three-piece from Charleston, South Carolina. When they played a cover of Björk's "Isobel," I felt a shiver run up my spine. There were probably only twelve people there, and it started to hit me as lead singer Dan McCurry whispered the vocals—"My name Isobel, married to myself"—we'd found something beautiful, something rare, something that didn't exist too often outside this town. We'd found a community of artists and fans and freaks, all of whom were trying to find a place in this world through their art.

Since then, I've fallen in love with this music scene. I moved just down the road to get my degree at the University of North Carolina, and the relationship only got more intricate in the years since I moved from my parents' home to my dorm room to my own apartment. Boyfriends have been fickle, majors have changed, but every weekend (and most week nights), there's a constant—a handful of venues with a handful of bands that end up surprising me time and time again.

There's something stirring and startling about the things that live music can do to your body and your brain. I've seen my favorite local bands more times than I can count, but with each new show, I'm stunned. Sometimes the most talented musicians in the area play to a crowd of ten. Sometimes, they play to a crowd of 150. Some of the best shows have been the least attended, but that's rarely the point. Most of the area's musicians know that even if they veer far out of left field, there will still be a place for them, a stage where a few people will shuffle their feet and listen with undivided attention.

As a journalist, I often ask myself this question: "What makes this music scene different from other towns?" In truth, I probably ask it because it's something I have so much trouble answering. I can't pinpoint that exact moment when I knew that the music that comes out of this place would make such an indelible impression on me. It was a slow and unconscious immersion, but here I am, irrevocably lovelorn, just like many others. What is it about this place that draws you in? What makes you turn down dates and walk to the Local 506 by your lonesome, all for the sake of a show? What about the chords of "Lalita" makes your spine tingle and your feet shuffle like they have minds of their own?

These are questions I still can't answer, probably because Chapel Hill and I have had such a lengthy and passionate tryst. But until I know the answers, I'll be standing at the Nightlight or the Local 506, an older version of the girl who found love in a low-ceilinged club.

LINNIE GREENE is a music journalist and former editor of "Diversions" at the *Daily Tar Heel*. She will graduate from the University of North Carolina at Chapel Hill in Spring 2012 with honors in Fiction. Until then, you can find her in area rock clubs until the wee hours of most mornings.

No Way

HARRY AMANA

CHAPEL HILL HAS GROWN ON ME over the three decades since I moved here in January 1979. It wasn't an easy transition. When I told friends and relatives back in Philadelphia that I had applied for a position in North Carolina, they gasped, "That's Jesse Helms's state." They were further alarmed when I later was chosen as a finalist for the job and was asked to come to Chapel Hill for an interview. "Don't go," some advised ominously.

I had been in North Carolina before. My mother's family was in New Bern, where we visited sometimes. I'd also stopped in a North Carolina town (maybe Rocky Mount) in August 1961 en route from Philadelphia to Fort Jackson, South Carolina, as a volunteer in the U.S. Army. I made the mistake of entering a train station eatery for whites only. . . . But that's another story.

And as a reporter in the mid-Seventies, I spent a day in Raleigh covering a national demonstration against racist repression in support of Ben Chavis and the Wilmington Ten, and death row resident Joan Little. I took photos of the demonstrators, of Central Prison, and of some local residents dressed in Klan robes who protested the protesters. Still *another* story.

But in early 1978—because of the huge cost of a last-minute plane trip to get to the interview at UNC—I took my second train ride to North Carolina, to Raleigh, which I thought was reasonably close to Chapel Hill. Wrong. The train arrived hours behind schedule, late at night. To get to Chapel Hill, a taxi was the *only* option.

When the cab left Raleigh, we embarked on a dark, empty Interstate 40. I became apprehensive. I remembered circuitous, touristy cab rides in Europe to get to hotels that, as it turned out, were half the distance the cabbies chose. But my driver assured me that I–40 was the fastest route to the university. He didn't tell me that the interstate had not yet been completed, and when we exited in Research Triangle Park and drove the rest of the way on a pitch-black, two-lane Highway 54, those Philadelphia warnings danced in my head.

At that point, the cab ride felt like some Star Trek ship sucked into a black worm hole. Nothing, I mean absolutely nothing of interest could be detected out the window—no development, few vehicles, an occasional closed gas station or small store, and trees! *Southern trees bear strange fruit / Blood on the leaves and blood at the root.* The lyrics from Billie Holiday's song rang in my ears. Where the hell was Chapel Hill?

When we finally arrived at the Carolina Inn and were greeted by black men in what appeared to be antebellum garb, I thought that the worm hole had dumped me somewhere in the mid-nineteenth century. Was I *really* going to be housed in that old plantation mansion? "This was a mistake," I thought. "There's no way I'm moving here, no way!"

That was my first view of Chapel Hill. It would be reinforced that night as I slept in a room unlike any hotel I had ever visited—more like a plantation bed and breakfast, homey and oh-so-folksy. And the next day I walked through the beautiful green campus, adorned with spacious quads canopied by huge trees while the campus bell tower chimes played dreamy plantation ditties. *No way!*

But decades later, here I am, having served twenty-eight years as a professor at the School of Journalism and Mass Communication. What happened?

What happened was Sonja Haynes Stone, and basketball—women's basketball. Stone was the legendary black professor who cofounded a cross-disciplinary journalism/black studies institute. I was there that day to interview for the position of the institute's director. My interview committee included Dr. Stone and representatives from Afro-American studies, the journalism school, the English department, and other university entities. It was an interracial group of progressive thinkers and scholars who genuinely seemed to like the university and its town, which boasted that it was a pat of butter in a sea of grits.

I didn't get that job—fundraising was a key part of it and I *hated* fundraising, as the committee quickly discovered. But Don Shaw, the journalism representative, asked if I would be interested in applying for a job at his shop. I was, I did, and I returned to Chapel Hill for an interview. I was hired for that position, which included being the liaison to Dr. Stone's institute.

Over time, I learned more about Chapel Hill's history: It was a relatively forward-thinking community that had elected a black mayor during the 1970s, had broken a campus speakers ban by having a Communist speaker stand on a public sidewalk and speak over a low wall *into* the campus, and whose basketball coach, Dean Smith, had broken the color barrier with the first black player in the ACC, Charlie Scott. The university also had an established press with a long history of publishing scholarly books on racial issues and a campus library that housed what is arguably the most extensive repository of materials on Southern history and culture.

Something else happened during my tenure here that made me fall in love with Chapel Hill. I discovered Carmichael Auditorium, the arena that hosts many of the women's sports activities. A beautiful field house— bathed in Carolina blue, with no bad seats—Carmichael literally vibrates with noise when the fans get busy. Even when there are only 3,000 fans there, it's a wonderful, three-ring circus. (Carmichael was the home of the men's teams before the Dean E. Smith Center was built.) And, like Duke's

Cameron Indoor Stadium or Philadelphia's Palestra, it's always been hard for visiting teams to win at Carmichael.

The fans are what really make this a truly Chapel Hill experience. School kids from Chapel Hill, Carrboro, and everywhere else in North Carolina come in droves, with teachers, parents, siblings, and friends. Many of them are girls. They wear their Carolina blue jerseys and T-shirts, shake pompoms, hoist handmade signs and banners, and have a field day. They know all the Tar Heel cheers and songs, their energy level is tuned to extreme, and their lungs are strong.

At the big games against perennially ranked teams like Duke, Connecticut, and Baylor, thousands of these energetic young people form what one local writer described as "one of the most devoted segments of the women's team's fan base." In 2003, they helped match a Carmichael record of 10,180, with standing room only.

I've been interested in women's basketball since the rules changed in the 1970s to allow them to play the same fast-paced version as the males. And I've been a UNC women's fanatic since Charlotte Smith (now a women's assistant coach) sank a rainbow three-pointer that won the NCAA championship game in 1994 by a single point at the buzzer. It's our first and only women's basketball championship, and the championship banner hangs auspiciously in Carmichael.

I point it out to my granddaughter, who plays basketball in Chapel Hill schools and goes to each of the games with me. "I know, Papaw Harry," she says, rolling her eyes and sighing. "You show it to me every time."

Down the street from Carmichael is the Sonja Haynes Stone Center for Black Culture and History, a stately building named after the late professor, who was instrumental in my moving to Chapel Hill. I experience a quiet, personal pride each time I see it. I was a member of the advisory board that wrote the proposal for the building. It is a symbol of change and hope.

Other things have changed. At the Carolina Inn, the plantation uniforms are gone. For more than three decades I have eaten at the inn's restaurant and attended scores of gatherings in its meeting rooms, ballrooms, and patios amidst much fellowship and camaraderie. And when my retirement party was held there a few years ago, I smiled to myself, thinking about my 1978 arrival. *No way!*

HARRY AMANA is an emeritus professor at the School of Journalism and Mass Communication at the University of North Carolina at Chapel Hill. He is the former director of the Sonja Haynes Stone Center for Black Culture and History. Parts of this essay were previously published in the *Chapel Hill News*.

The Religion of the Forehead

(Selections from *To Hate Like This Is to Be Happy Forever*)

WILL BLYTHE

RAISING HIS CHILDREN in the International Brotherhood of Duke Haters was the natural and one of the more enjoyable aspects of my father's master plan, though "plan" is probably too intentional a word for the improvisations of child rearing. His intent, let us say, was to develop his children into good Southerners of the North Carolinian persuasion. He wanted us to embody the values of our family, going back generations. To an observer, a foreigner in our midst (say, like me), it may have appeared that my father intended to turn us into younger versions of himself.

But there were obstacles. My siblings and I were growing up in Chapel Hill, a university town in which cosmopolitan toxins pervaded the air like the odor of dogwood blossoms. Or was it the scent of Thai stick? Ours was the town that Senator Jesse Helms had suggested surrounding with a chain-link fence in order to build the state zoo. Or so we liked to brag. It wasn't necessary to go to New England every summer and visit my mother's family to absorb dangerous diction, hard consonants, and mean vowels. That could come to us every day from our teachers and coaches and friends and their families, and from that demonic television set in the breakfast room that spoke a liltless tongue called Middle American.

And so began our supper-table lessons in how to talk right. Notice that I said "supper," not "dinner." North Carolinians of my father's generation did not sit down to dinner at night. They sat down to supper. Dinner took place in the middle of the day.

"How do you say F-O-R-E-H-E-A-D?" my father asked us many a supper, spelling out the word lest he give away the answer. He and my mother sat at opposite ends of the kitchen table with the four children between them, my sister, Annie, and I on one side, my brothers, John and David, on the other. My mother listened to the interrogation with bemused and anxious forbearance. My father monitored our answers like a detective taking a suspect's statement.

"F-O-R-E-H-E-A-D. Come on. How do you say it?"

Most Americans these days would answer *for-head*, rhyming the word with *oar-head*. But that was not the answer my father was seeking. That was wrong. Only ignorant barbarians said *for-head*. Or people from other states, who probably had no choice but to be ignorant barbarians. We had a choice.

Sooner or later, someone (the younger siblings usually succumbed first) would chime in with the correct response, which was *far-red*, the first syllable rhyming with *tar*, which was appropriate for young Tar Heels like ourselves. To answer otherwise, as I sometimes did out of sheer perversity and because in fact my father was teaching us how to stand our ground in the larger world (I just applied the lesson at home, too), was to witness him shake his head mournfully and tell us (me) that we just had to rebel, a tendency which must have come from my mother's side. Why couldn't we just accept the truth of certain things, like the proper way to say F-O-R-E-H-E-A-D, instead of disputing or making fun of them?

I sometimes ventured that a word might be pronounced one way in one part of the country and differently in another. He would tell me that in the case of F-O-R-E-H-E-A-D I was wrong. And that even if I had been right, it was hurtful to the discriminating ear to hear *for-head* rather than *far-red*.

"How do you pronounce F-L-O-R-I-D-A?" he asked.

"*Flar-da.*" Resistance was useless.

"F-O-R-E-S-T?"

"*Far-rest.*"

"That's the ticket! Hotcha!" Oh, how happy he was when we gave him the pronunciation for which he yearned. He beamed with family happiness. He ushered us warmly into the exclusive club of good North Carolinians, true Southerners.

"You all seem so close," more than one person has said about my siblings and me.

"We had a common oppressor," I tell them.

And yet, drilled though we were, watched over like prisoners in the yard, hectored and pursued like lovers who might spurn their suitor for another (for that is what this was really all about), I understand now with great sympathy what my tyrannical father was after. He wanted his children to be able to speak with the ghosts of our ancestors, to preserve through language a realm outside of time. He desired that we speak that ancient tongue to him. And in doing things in the old way, we would link ourselves to family members both dead and gone and yet to come. Saying "forehead" was like lighting a candle in our religion.

And so was hating Duke. It was part of who we were, how we defined ourselves in a world unmoored.

The Betrayal

ON CHRISTMAS DAY, 2004, we gathered around our balding tree, opened presents, and remembered Christmases past. My father's absence was still palpable; we missed his joy in the yearly rituals, his fireside sermons on the religion of family and home. He had regarded my life in New York as a betrayal, one forced perhaps by circumstances, but a treachery nonetheless. In his eyes, my domicile made my credentials as a Southerner somewhat suspect. All I had to do was eat supper at eight o'clock—"New York hours," he grumbled—and I was a turncoat. A true Southerner ate supper at 6:30, which, as it happened, was when my father liked to eat.

One Christmas in the late Nineties, not long before he died, I sat across from him in the living room, both of us arrayed in the same positions we'd taken twenty-five years before, during The Years of Teenage Rebellion. I can't recall why (maybe it was the punch we were consuming, which contained four different types of liquor), but for some reason, I started enumerating the things I missed about North Carolina. There wasn't anything exceptional about my list. It included such Southern staples as the sound of June bugs on a blistering July afternoon; the politeness to be had at the 7-Eleven, where the manager was always ready to pass the time of day with you at the expense of speedy service; and the slow-cooked wisdom of the state's old liberal avatars, such as Judge Dickson Phillips, a friend of my father's whom we both admired. Judge Phillips had once cut through my angst at deciding where to go to college by asking me a simple question: "Will, are you a happy person?" I suspected that I might be, and I told him so. "Well then, you'll be happy wherever you go," the judge said. Case closed. Time to watch football.

My father listened quietly as I talked that night, and I thought nothing more of the conversation until the next morning, when he came to the bedroom where my wife and I were packing to head back to New York. He stood at the door, watching us and weeping.

My wife and I looked up from the suitcase we were at the moment coincidentally stuffing with MoonPies, a nutritious Southern staple made of marshmallows, chocolate, and all sorts of delicious hydrogenated grease that I liked to bestow upon my friends and coworkers in New York. The easiest place for me to be a Southerner, I had discovered, was in Manhattan. Give a Yankee a MoonPie and they look at me like I am Robert E. Lee. Or Hank Williams. Or Bear Bryant. "What is it?" they ask.

"Why, chile, that's a MoonPie," I say.

"What's in it?"

"I can't tell you what's in it. But I can tell you that it'll put hair on your chest and lead in your pencil."

So here we were, packing our MoonPie contraband into our luggage, and here was my father at the door, crying. "I wish all of you could live down here," he said. He had frequently offered us a patch of land behind the house, a little perch on the hillside, where he hoped we would build a residence and establish a compound of Blythes, all within hollering distance of one another.

"I wish we could, too," I said.

"That meant a lot to me, what you said about North Carolina last night," he said. "I didn't know you felt that way."

"Well, I do," I said.

"Why don't you move back, then?" he asked.

"Can't right now. Work and all. But I'd like to."

"I don't know about that. I doubt you're ever coming back," my father said. Now he was returning to another one of his roles: skeptical victim of his children's incomprehensible decisions. The King Lear of 114 Hillcrest Circle. He turned to trudge down the hallway, the tears still pearled on his cheeks, his frame looking suddenly smaller and swallowed-up in his khaki pants and his worn white shirt with its sleeves rolled up to his elbows.

The Family That Hates Together

A FAMILY THAT PLAYS together is a family that stays together, but a family that hates together is a family that really loves each other, everyone glopped together like a ball of sticky rice. Let me show you what I mean. It is game night this season at the Blythe household. Through the wind-swayed winter woods, the lights of University Mall flit and twinkle in the distance.

Inside, Sheba the dog slumbers on the rug in the TV room. But as tip-off approaches, she hauls herself into the kitchen in anticipation of the tumult to come. Like many animal species, dogs are said to have a sixth sense when it comes to impending earthquakes.

There on the sofa to the right of the TV is my mother, silver-haired and dignified, more kindhearted than anyone I have ever known. Her bills and church-circle correspondence are stacked beside her, and if North Carolina's lead is a comfortable one (for her, around 40 or 50 points), she might even get a little work done. She is a good Presbyterian woman. And she hates Duke.

On the big sofa across the rug from my mother, you will find my sister, the reporter. Objectivity is her middle name. She lectures me about being faithful to facts. She is concerned that I might play too loose with them. I tell her she is a real journalist and she is kind to be concerned but that I am something else. When she's not writing her objective accounts of local citizens, my sister lives the genteel life of a gardener, tending her flowers and trees, worrying over her peppers and tomatoes. She might say about herself that she is naturally shy but that she has learned how to talk to people, which indeed she has. She cooks an occasional meal for my mother and me, and in my time in New York has become an extraordinary cook. How did this happen? Soon, my shy, pepper-growing sister will unleash upon the television set a harangue that would brush back Don Rickles. She, too, hates Duke.

I sit next to my sister on the big couch, though "sitting" is an imprecise term for what I actually do. For me, the next couple of hours will be all about the positioning, about the spin I can put on the game by contorting my body into necessary postures. Really, it all depends on the flow of the game. As coaches like to say, you shouldn't decide all of your tactics ahead of time. You need to remain sensitive to every shift in the action. So, as you can see, I am a reasonable man. I try to do right in this world. But I, too, hate Duke.

Were my brothers, David and John, available, they, too, would cluster here, one on the rug, one parked next to my mother. Wives, girlfriends, children moving in and out of the room: They knew that this was not their fight and that it was hopeless to try and impose normal standards of etiquette on the proceedings.

One family, united in the dark sacrament of disdain, facing the world together, side by side, couch by couch. We've got each other's backs and we're ready for the game to begin.

The Beast Is Alive

TONIGHT WE ARE WATCHING DUKE PLAY CLEMSON. We are monitoring our adversary for cracks, structural defects, familial dysfunction. We want to know who mopes, who snaps under pressure, who misses. We are scholars of the slippery slope, the January weaknesses that portend doom in March—the point guard who can't shoot, the two guard who can't defend, the center who clanks free throws.

The new year has arrived but when it comes to hatred, the beast is already in midseason form. He lives not just in me, his favorite host, but in my mother and my sister.

"How can anyone stand to look at him?" my mother asks, staring at Mike Krzyzewski.

"It's a mystery to me," my sister says. "One that is simply beyond our human capacity to understand."

"My friend Nina Wallace can read lips," my mother says. "She says you ought to *see* the kinds of things he says."

These are the kind of things we say. The game is ugly, too. At one point, the commentator compares it to a root canal. Both teams are building a brick wall of missed shots. With 7:34 to play in the first half, the score is deadlocked at an unimpressive 10 to 10.

The second half is more of the same: turnovers, fouls, neither team shooting over 35 percent. "Why do they get to foul so much?" my sister asks of the Blue Devils.

"Because they're Duke," my mother says.

"That's another one of those profound mysteries," I tell my sister.

"Sit down," my mother instructs Mike Krzyzewski.

"Miss!" I shout at Lee Melchionni. His three-pointer ripples through the net and he runs down the court, fists clenched, screaming.

"They're so lucky," my sister says.

"I hate the way he screams after every shot," I say.

Clemson makes a game of it, pounding the boards. The Tigers actually take a 38-to-35 lead midway through the second half. Our misanthropic band cheers. "Whip their sorry asses," I say.

My mother appears to suppress a smile. She doesn't ordinarily like that kind of language, but there is a time and a place for everything. "Come on, fellas," she says to the Tigers, which I think is her way of saying something similar.

"Wouldn't it be great if they won?" my sister says.

But they don't. JJ Redick scores 20 of his 24 points in the second half. He's not bashful about putting it up, even though he's only four of 11 from three, eight of 19 from the field overall.

"They don't look that good," I say.

"They're beatable," my sister says.

"I hope you're right," my mother says. "Because I can't stand them." That's our family. Sweet right up until tip-off.

I remember the spring afternoon my girlfriend watched me in horror as I ventilated my darker passions while watching Duke play Carolina. I sought to quell her anxiety. "I'm having fun," I told her.

"That's what that is?" she asked.

"Yes, most assuredly," I said.

"I don't think I'd want to see you not having fun," she said.

"But you have," I said. "It looks sort of like this but different."

"Right," she said.

"The key thing is not to take it personally," I reassured her.

"I don't."

"Good. You shouldn't."

"Your whole family," she said. "They seem so civilized. So nice."

"They are," I said. "They're really nice."

"But when you guys watch basketball . . ."

"Yeah, I know. That's when the beast comes out."

Listen, I'm not really justifying this. I'm explaining, not excusing. I mean, there's a reason or two, or maybe a couple of dozen, why I am this way.

Mostly, I'm well-behaved as a journalist ought to be. Mostly, I am studying myself and those around me from a cool, interstellar distance. It's curious how this Duke-hating and Carolina-loving became so intense.

But every now and then, I can't help it. The old impulses reemerge. I watch a game and I go bonkers. It seems the whole universe is tied in to the game. But I worry that by such deep immersion in this obsession over the next few months, I may start to dissolve it. That can happen—it's the smoke-ten-packs-of-cigarettes-the-day-before-you-quit theory of killing an addiction. I can't quite imagine life without basketball, however.

I told this to a friend and she said, "Oh, that's good. Maybe this will cure you somehow."

"But I don't want to be cured," I said.

The Pleasures of Hatred

AT TIMES IT TROUBLES ME a little to be so full of piss and vinegar. A man of my age ought to be seasoning into acceptance like a salt-cured ham. The study I've done of Buddhist literature (such study being much easier than the actual practice of Buddhism) suggests that not only is hatred bad on a cosmic level, but it is also bad for us personally. We are going to pay for our bad deeds and our evil thoughts by being reincarnated again and again, swirled from one life to another like dirty clothes on endless spin cycle. Although it isn't very Buddhist of me to worry about ending in the karmic washer for a few billion extra millennia merely because *I* have the odd hateful thought—I should be more concerned with others ending up in such straits—I can't help but fret about my fate. One North Carolina–Duke game alone probably costs me several millennia of rebirths.

And yet, how I hate.

From across the centuries, I recently found good company in the English essayist William Hazlitt, who died back in 1830, nearly friend-less, it is true, and with hardly a tuppence in his pocket. But no one ever said hatred is the best way of winning a man friends and money. Samuel Coleridge, one of Hazlitt's erstwhile friends, described him as "ninety-nine in a hundred singularly repulsive." Hazlitt's wife left him on returning from their honeymoon. And yet as he lay dying in a tiny room, Hazlitt said, "Well, I've had a happy life."

Could hatred, like prayer or Prozac, have been the secret? In 1826, Hazlitt wrote an essay called "On the Pleasure of Hating," a profound work that expresses what we might call a holistic view of hatred. He puts the noblest face possible on a snarl. "Nature seems made up of antipathies," he proposes. "Without something to hate, we should lose the very spring of thought and action." This struck me as quite likely—that every bit as much as love, hatred moved a person to ponder and to act. And that such hatred needn't even be personal. It might be disdain for injustice, for poverty, for drunk driving. Hate the sin, not the sinner. Or so it seemed upon first reading. Things actually got more complicated.

Hazlitt had detected the boredom inherent in goodness, the totalitarian features of the standard-issue heaven. "Pure good soon grows insipid, wants variety and spirit," he writes. "Pain is a bittersweet, which never surfeits. Love turns, with a little indulgence, to indifference or disgust: hatred alone is immortal." I knew marriages like that, kept alive, if not flourishing, by endless campaigns of attack and counterattack, animosity an apparently inexhaustible fuel of togetherness.

Hazlitt's final estimation of the dynamics of hatred, "the wild beast," proves fascinating. Hatred alights on conditions such as injustice to express itself. Hazlitt takes a swipe at religion as one of the prime venues for this basic human need for antagonism. "What have the different sects, creeds, doctrines in religion been but so many pretexts set up for men to wrangle, to quarrel, to tear one another in pieces . . . ?"

The author expresses himself in that English manner we've come to think of as commonsensical. "Public nuisances," he writes, "are in the nature of public benefits." That is, they not only excite the body politic, they sting it into collectivity. "How long did the Pope, the Bourbons, and the Inquisition keep the people of England in breath, and supply them with nicknames to vent their spleen upon!" Had they done us any harm of lately? No: but we have always a quantity of superfluous bile upon the stomach, and we wanted an object to let it out upon.

Yes! I know just how that misanthrope felt. Substitute Duke for the Pope, et al., and, well, Duke had sopped up a lot of superfluous bile in my day. In the early Nineties, for instance, I seemed to have hated Bobby Hurley, the short and skinny Duke point guard. Yes, frail Bobby Hurley, whom by all rights I should have identified with for his striving against the odds, his fearless adventures in the lane among the giants. Bobby Hurley who cried when North Carolina point guard King Rice muscled him around his freshman season.

Hurley even made certain American virtues suspect because he was the one embodying them. Grit, for instance. Hurley definitely had grit. You didn't need Dick Vitale to point it out a thousand times. You could see it yourself, watching this New Jersey white kid blaze up and down the court like a Chevy Camaro about to throw a rod. He drove the lane with the bony éclat of an overachiever unafraid of a pounding. And at least he cared enough to cry.

Let me be the first to admit that had Bobby Hurley played for UNC, as he had wanted to do before Dean Smith told him he would have to wait for high school star Kenny Anderson to decide where he wanted to attend college, I might have seen those defects for the virtues they can be. Hatred, therefore, teaches us that context is everything. Our passions are fickle; they'll enlist in whatever battle we care to fight.

I have come to believe that worse than an honest hate is a dishonest piety. How much further from heaven is such a posture.

The former literary editor of *Esquire*, **WILL BLYTHE** is the author of *To Hate Like This Is to Be Happy Forever*, excerpted here. A frequent contributor to the *New York Times Book Review*, he has written for numerous publications, including the *New Yorker*, *Rolling Stone*, and *Sports Illustrated*, and his work has been anthologized in *The Best American Short Stories* and *The Best American Sportswriting*.

Friends & Neighbors ❧

Poetic Justice

ERICA EISDORFER

I LIVED IN THREE DIFFERENT HOUSES on Justice Street in Chapel Hill which is something of a feat considering that it's only two blocks long. It gets its name from Charlie "Choo Choo" Justice, UNC's favorite football player. He played back when they wore leather football helmets. I don't much care for football but I do like Justice Street.

I had been living in Durham for four years, in a house with no indoor plumbing, when my boyfriend at the time asked me to move to Chapel Hill where, he said, they have flush toilets. This seemed like a reasonable request and, since I'd long since proved my haleness, I agreed to it. I rented a room in Justice Street House #1 which was a Quonset hut with a room tacked on either end. The house was shingled and charming and verminous. All manner of reptile, insect, and small mammal life lived within its walls. Once, as I watched, a possum climbed out of a kitchen cabinet. This was country Chapel Hill. My roommate and I were like pioneers, fighting back fauna at every turn.

Twenty-five years later, Chapel Hill's still mighty country. On my carpool mornings, my daughter and I look for the cow with the dog-shaped spot in the field across from her school. If the dog-shaped spot is turned away, you have to try harder all day long. I like that my kid goes to school across from a cow field. It sustains my abiding hope for as much pasture as possible.

Sarah, my roommate in the Quonset hut, had a boyfriend who worked at an organic grocery store, building kaleidoscopic vegetable displays. He also juggled. His name was Simcha Weinstein, which seemed sort of town to me because you don't really think of Jews as country folk. Jews seem urban. This is because of the Pale of Settlement in Catherine's Russia, when Jews weren't allowed to own land which is why they became lawyers and merchants. Years before he met my roommate, and despite his name, Simcha had been ordained as a minister by mail-order, so that he could perform weddings for his friends back on the commune. Back then, Chapel Hill was full of hippies. In the Sixties and Seventies, Franklin Street was lined with hippies selling leather crafts and bongs which gave it a sort of funky, edgy feel and which resulted in the moniker "the Greenwich Village of the South." That's why, when my father took us on a sabbatical to San Francisco in 1969, I didn't immediately expire from culture shock.

When Simcha and Sarah got married, I found another roommate. She was the sister of my best friend's partner whom I'd met because I worked with another brother of theirs whose wife came over to play Trivial Pursuit and felt that her brother-in-law and my best friend would make a perfect couple. I now employ the daughter of one of the above couples. The preceding is an example of Chapel Hill as village. Family connections are as prized here as if we're all living in the time of Eleanor of Aquitaine.

I moved out of the Quonset hut in part because I was tired of sharing the house with creatures that had more legs than I did and partly because I was pregnant and wanted to live by myself to prepare for never living by myself again. House #2, on the other block of Justice Street, was teensy. Me and my belly made it very snug. The cat I adopted immediately ran away which was just as well because of the space he took up. After Sophie was born, I saw him again. He'd taken up residence at the Quonset hut despite the fact that he'd never lived there before. Now that I think upon it, that house needed a cat. Sophie, who is now twenty-one, is good friends with a young woman who lives in that Quonset hut and visits her often. I've never heard her remark on the crawly nature of the house and think that perhaps the cat took care of the problem once and for all.

I made friends with JD, the young woman who rented the house next door to House #2. The house belonged to a writer who was busy teaching at Sarah Lawrence in New York. My mother had met the writer some years earlier and instantly loved him. She recalled that riding the subway as a young woman, she read a story in the *New Yorker* by a young writer whose prospects she liked. His name was John Updike. "I felt the same way," she said, "when I read Allan's story in the *New Yorker*." Annually, my mother and I go to New York to attend the New Yorker Festival. There, we listen to panels of authors and politicos. Recently, we spoke to the people in line with us. "I'm from Chicago," said the guy in front of us. "I'm from Montreal," said the woman in back of us. "I'm from Chapel Hill," said I, refusing to qualify, as if it were Paris I lived in, or maybe New York itself.

JD, the young woman who lived in the writer's house next door, had a pregnant dog. The dog and I went into labor on the same night. I preferred to stay at home until I absolutely had to go to the hospital, but the house was so small that there wasn't room for me to pace so I paced outside in the driveway. Meanwhile, Murphy the dog was in the writer's shed, ten feet away, birthing her puppies. The whole situation reminded me of a nature documentary.

When Sophie was about a year old, House #3 opened up right across the street. It had, as an advantage, enough space to walk in. My new next-door neighbor was an environmentalist who shunned the idea of the lawn and devoted the whole of the considerable green space in front of his house to beautiful meadow. He ought to have kept a cow but there's probably an ordinance against cows in town, though if the city fathers had walked over from Town Hall, they might have thought they were in the heart of the country and changed their minds just this once. There were, however, plenty of bluebirds which apparently prefer a meadow to just about anything. Once, while talking to my brother Marco over the phone, he identified a bluebird in my front yard. "See if you can spot it, Erica," he said from where he sat in Bloomington, Indiana. "It sounds like it's in front of you, and maybe to the left." It was.

House #2 is where Sophie and I lived when Marco died of AIDS. Not long after he died, I went to see Bill T. Jones, a New York choreographer who wrote about AIDS and who had come to Chapel Hill to perform. I stood in line to meet him and hugged him and cried, which probably happened to him a lot but he was very nice about it. Meanwhile, a beloved Chapel Hill chef, whose destination-restaurant urbanized grits enough for even the biggest city slickers, was dying of it. And my neighbor, the writer, was in the midst of a novel about AIDS in New York, a novel in which he used my brother as the model for one of the minor characters, whose name was Marco and who knew all there was to know about birds. City had landed on the village; the village stooped under the burden but some of us survived.

After Marco's death, one of his friends from Bloomington and I began to write to each other. We fell in love through the mail. Dave moved down to be with Sophie and me and then, a year or so later, we married. We asked Simcha to perform the ceremony. He was perfect. His name was Weinstein for my dad; he was a minister for Dave's mom. We married under a big tree on the lawn of the Horace Williams House, named after a professor of philosophy at UNC who thought a lot about justice. People came from city and countryside to be with us. Allan told us later that the birds sang so loudly, we could hardly get a word in edgewise.

ERICA EISDORFER is the author of *The Wet Nurse's Tale*. She is the longtime manager of the Bull's Head Bookshop at the University of North Carolina at Chapel Hill.

Muslims in the Cul-de-sac

SAMIA SERAGELDIN

IN THE RHYTHM OF THE SEASONS, Fall is the true beginning of the year in a college town. In the South, in particular, the cooler, crisper breezes of September dispel the lethargy of the long, muggy summer months, and the bustle of returning students jolts the sleepy downtown streets back to life. Just as the song of the scarlet cardinals heralds the renewal of Spring, the influx of students pouring into campus heralds a new academic year.

So it was always in September that I organized my annual open house in the college town I had called home for ten years. A "wine and heavy hors d'oeuvres" affair, it was an occasion to reconnect with a diverse group of returning summer wanderers: colleagues from the university and the local newspaper, French and Francophile friends from conversation groups. I invited about thirty people, no RSVP required, and estimated that about twenty-five would show up.

That September of the first year of the new millennium, my only source of concern was the weather: A friend had offered to help with landscaping the yard, and as it turned out, could only do it on the day of the party itself, a Saturday. "Don't worry," Karen reassured me. "It will all be done before your guests arrive at seven." I wondered if she had bitten off more than she could chew. The previous weekend, a mound of mulch as high as the house had been delivered and sat in my driveway, and bushes in canvas sacks lined the path to the front door. If it rained before Saturday, there would be an unholy mess.

As I checked my email the Tuesday before the party, I kept glancing out the window at the pile of mulch and at the sky, praying the good weather would last through the weekend. A box suddenly opened on my screen, flashing what looked like a trailer for a disaster movie: black smoke pouring out of tall buildings. Then the phone rang. "Turn on the television," a friend instructed grimly. The World Trade Center towers had been attacked.

My first thought was for my older son, who regularly had business in downtown New York. I couldn't reach him. My second thought was to pray that the perpetrators, as it turned out with the Oklahoma bombing, were not from the Middle East. My third thought was for the friends who had children or relatives in New York, and I tried to call them.

When it seemed increasingly likely that the hijackers were Middle Eastern, my reaction was to get up, tidy the house, and do the laundry. That instinct, I realize now, was more atavistic than rational. Growing up in Egypt, whenever there was a national catastrophe, like the 1967 defeat, my father and uncles packed their overnight bags, preparing to be hauled away by the Intelligence Service, the Mukhabarat, simply because they were on the list of "enemies of the people."

I didn't pack an overnight bag, but I prepared for some inchoate eventuality: that our house would be searched by the FBI, or that neighbors might come to the door. It seemed important for everything to be tidy and clean, laundry done and put away, the house presentable, ready for inspection. As if, from that moment on, I had lost the right to privacy, the right not to be judged as a representative of a perceived community.

I told my younger son to pick up his room and take down his laundry. For once, he obeyed without question, and the full significance of that struck me later.

As I picked up the books trailing about all over the house and stuffed them back on the shelves, I turned the spines of the few books in Arabic toward the bookcase.

But at least having something with which to occupy myself broke the unbearable paralysis that bound me to the television set and the telephone. When my older son finally called—from Hong Kong, as it happened— I breathed again. But then my thought was for the mothers who did not receive that reassuring phone call.

There was no knock on the door from police or neighbors that day or the days that followed. There was a phone call from a French journalist in New York; she had been sent to cover the attack on the towers and to wrap up her coverage with a report from "heartland America." We had French friends in common who had suggested Chapel Hill as a location and gave her my number as a local contact. I said I would help any way I could. She would be arriving Saturday.

Saturday! The day of the open house. Should I cancel? But how? I had invited people weeks ahead, and since I had not asked for an RSVP, I had no idea who might actually attend. I contemplated calling one by one every-one I had invited and disinviting them, but I couldn't remember everybody. What would it look like to the neighbors if I held a party—to which none of them, incidentally, had been invited? Not that I didn't get along with the neighbors, only that we had little in common and didn't socialize. For one thing, my children were grown, and most of the families in the cul-de-sac had bought their houses from the original owners and had much younger children; the turnover was pretty high among families of young profession-als, what with the booming economy of Research Triangle Park nearby.

I worried that a frenzy of landscaping and partying would look to the neighbors at the very least like ghastly insensitivity to the terrible events earlier that week. I worried and worried, but given the impracticality of can-celing, I finally decided to go ahead, expecting that few people would show up anyway, if for no other reason than because they were in no mood to tear themselves away from the horror show that was our television screens.

Every time the phone rang I wondered if it would be someone calling to cancel or confirm, but there were neither. There was a call, out of the blue, from the parents of a college friend of my son's, a successful, jolly couple, also one of the most fervently Christian families I knew. The parents, whom we'd only met a couple of times at college events, were calling to let us know that if we felt in any way threatened or uncomfortable, we were welcome to stay at their beach house for as long as we liked. We reassured them that there was no cause for concern. Their genuine kindness touched me to tears, but the justifiable assumption behind the gesture depressed me.

Saturday morning Karen showed up with her sleeves rolled up and a couple of men to do the heavy lifting. I pitched in, ineffectively, and she chased me indoors to set up for the party. The pile of mulch gradually diminished, as the neighbors went about their weekend business, eyeing the activity with curious glances.

But I had a strategy: to corner Gwen, my neighbor across the street, the only survivor, other than me, of the original residents of the cul-de-sac when it was a new subdivision ten years earlier. It wouldn't be hard to run into Gwen; she made it her business to know what was going on, perhaps in her capacity as doyenne of the neighborhood. Gwen and her husband, a researcher in physics at the university, were childless; but she always had a reason to hang about her front yard, and you could hear her speaking to various neighbors, mailmen, and delivery people in a Minnesota accent that carried effortlessly across the entire block.

Gwen could be counted on to relay any information you wished to publicize. So the Saturday of the party, I saw her taking her time looking through her mail at the bottom of her driveway, and went over and explained that the landscaping, and the party, had been planned a month ago and that I had no way of canceling. She nodded encouragingly. Message delivered.

A quarter of an hour before the guests arrived, Karen packed up her gear and her crew and left, promising to come back when she had showered and changed.

The French journalist was the first to arrive, a little before seven: a thirty-something brunette, wearing combat boots with her denim skirt; perhaps she had prepared for ground zero, or perhaps it was just urban chic. We discussed various venues were I could help her set up interviews: Duke University, where I taught at the time; the newspaper, where I contributed a weekly book review column; the sole Afghan restaurant in the area, Bread and Kabob.

"Oh, and tomorrow is Sunday, I would like to attend a service at a Protestant church. It must be a *Protestant* church," Valérie—that was her name—stressed.

"What kind of Protestant church?" I asked.

Just then the doorbell rang. I looked at my watch: It was seven fifteen.
Joan, an old friend, walked through the open door carrying a paper bag of the latest overflow from her vegetable garden. Valérie jumped up and stuck a small mic in her face. "Hi! I'm Valérie. I'm doing a *reportage* on the reaction to the attacks. May I ask where were you when you heard?"

Joan recoiled. I apologized and asked Valérie not to ambush my guests that way. By seven thirty people began to arrive in clusters, and by eight there were thirty-five people hanging about the kitchen and the living room and overflowing onto the deck. Some of my friends, bless them, had even brought friends of theirs along. I was still too unused to the new order of things to fully appreciate their kindness.

Before she left I asked Valérie if she had any particular denomination of Protestant church in mind for the Sunday service and she said no, just Protestant. I asked her to come by the next morning at eleven and we went to attend the service at the brand new evangelical church down the street. It was a convenient five-minute walk and it fulfilled her criterion. For weeks I had seen the posters advertising the grand opening on Sunday, September 16.

Valérie was visibly impressed as we walked across the vast parking lot to the front of the enormous, circular edifice that could be mistaken for a sports stadium. Inside she was even more taken aback by the raised sound stage on which a band of musicians were tuning up while a giant screen overhead projected video clips of young evangelists on their missions — the church catered mostly to university students. I talked to the pastor, a good-looking, forty-something man with a resolutely cheerful manner, and he promised an interview for Valérie after the service. We took our seats in the front row of the stadium-style circular benches.

I had brought a hat with me, but no one else was wearing one, so I kept it in my lap; the woman sitting behind me leaned forward and whispered archly: "Pretty hat; but if you want to wear that, you'll have to go to a black church."

"Qu'est-ce qu'elle dit?" Valérie hissed; fluent in English though she was, Southern accents foiled her. But she switched on her little tape recorder and recorded it all, the music and the clapping and the dancing, and the solemn moment when the pastor asked everyone assembled to stand up and hold hands and pray — for victory for the university's football team that season. We were all at the time, I realize now, still in the denial stage of grief.

But as the weeks turned into months, denial turned to anger. In the battery of funhouse images of Islam that blared from television, radio, and newspapers headlines, I could not recognize the faith with which I was raised. Wherever I turned, it was bewildering and inescapable. When it became unbearable, I knew I needed to act. If you had a choice — and I did — you could keep a low profile and blend in as you always had, or you could stand up and speak out. I think my choice was decided from the moment I told my son to pick up his room and he obeyed without question.

I called the librarian at the town library, where I had recently been invited to give a reading for my first novel, and offered to give a talk about Islam. She discussed it with the board and called me back to say that they would take me up on my offer and would schedule me for the Sunday after next, as part of their regular Meet the Author events; except, she stressed, that they would not be serving the usual coffee and cookies. I understood perfectly: They could not be seen as in any way endorsing whatever it was I had to say.

Even without the lure of refreshments, sixty people showed up for my talk, a record for the Sunday series, and the session ran well over the allotted time. Questions ran the gamut from genuine curiosity to barely disguised hostility. At the conclusion I felt that at least no one had left with a worse impression than they had when they arrived, and several people came up to me and asked if I would speak at their church.

I think it must have been the third or fourth church—a Presbyterian congregation—at which I was speaking when I caught sight of my neighbor Gwen in the audience; she actually seemed to duck when I tried to make eye contact. After the talk I caught her at the coatrack by the door.

"Why Gwen, is this your church?"

"No, I go to the Lutheran church. But I'm in charge of adult education programs for my church and I'm organizing a series of speakers on Islam, so I came to hear you. Actually I didn't know it was you, just that they would have a Muslim speaker. I didn't know we had Muslims in the cul-de-sac!"

And there it was, the phrase I was to remember so often afterward: Muslims in the cul-de-sac.

"But Gwen, we've been neighbors for eight years, what did you think we were?"

"I don't know. But I didn't think you were that sort of Muslim!"

What sort of Muslim did she mean? The type, presumably, who didn't wear shorts and a tank top to water the bushes, and didn't have parties after which the recycle bin put out on the curb was full of empty wine bottles? But I never found out what she meant. Other people were edging around to ask me questions, and she left.

Gwen came to my door the next day with a stack of magazines. "Do you know this magazine?" She held up a copy of *Aziza* with an African American woman in a headscarf on the cover.

"No, I don't actually."

"Oh, I thought you would. It's for Muslim women. I've been subscribing to it for a few weeks now, since I'm organizing the speaker series on Islam."

I thought of our African American mailman with his habitual smile, and how it must confuse him to deliver *Aziza* to Gwen. I asked her to come in. She had only been in my house once before, to an open house I gave when we first moved in, but as she never reciprocated, I didn't repeat the invitation. But after that terrible September, whenever Gwen, or anyone for that matter, came to my door, I invited them in: I felt an obligation to show that my life was an open book.

Over the next couple of weeks Gwen came many times with questions about Islam, and to ask for advice about speakers. So far she had invited only non-Muslim scholars of religion; she was ready to take the next step and invite a Muslim to speak, but was worried about some nasty email from members of her congregation accusing her of wanting to bring terrorists to the church.

Gwen finally went ahead and invited me to her church—but not to her home. That was to happen much later, and it was to be the first and the last time.

For Gwen's sake, I hope I did a good job before her congregation that day; it seemed to go smoothly enough. I remember one man who kept mentioning that I had soft hands, which baffled me until I understood he was trying to make the point that he had shaken hands with me earlier, in contravention to what he had apparently been told to expect from Muslim women.

These talks I gave, sometimes as often as twice a week, were a strain, but I welcomed them for the temporary relief from helplessness they provided. Like many people, I lost a year of my life, numbly watching HGTV or the Food Network when I could no longer bear the news channels. I wanted my old life back.

Pulling in and out of our driveway became fraught with a certain tension. I realized that I had been guilty of the one failing people rarely forgive: lack of curiosity about them. I had been the kind of oblivious neighbor who pulls into and out of her garage with her mind on other things, barely sparing a distracted glance for who might be about or what was going on. Now I noticed everything. The neighbors didn't wave, but then perhaps they never had? The children in particular seemed sullen and suspicious as they paused in their pick-up ball games to let my car through; but perhaps that was my imagination? The minor sources of friction — inconsiderate neighbors who let their dogs mess in our yard, or blew their leaves onto our lawn, or parked on the curb in front of our mailbox, blocking the postman's access — I let it all go. Perhaps I would have anyway.

That was around the time Attorney General John Ashcroft encouraged Americans, as a civic duty, to spy on "suspicious" neighbors, and mailmen, gas-meter readers, and other utility workers were exhorted to take advantage of their access and snoop about the premises. I never seriously considered that any of my neighbors, not even the least friendly, and certainly not our smiling, long-time mailman, would be that paranoid.

Before the invasion of Iraq, Gwen came around again for one of our sessions. She asked if it was possible the Iraqi people might welcome the invasion, given how much they must hate Saddam. I thought of the Suez crisis of 1956; at the time Egypt was attacked, if anyone had a reason to wish for the toppling of Nasser's regime and the restoration of the status quo ante, it would have been my father: The coup d'état of the colonels had stripped our family of its fortunes and his eldest brother was imprisoned. But my father was a nationalist; far from harboring the hope that the invasion would succeed, he volunteered for civil defense. I didn't go into all that with Gwen, needless to say.

One day Gwen waylaid me as I was pulling into my driveway. But this time she didn't have a question about Islam or Iraq; she wanted to tell me that she was getting divorced from her husband of eighteen years. I was touched, and surprised, that I was the one she chose to confide in; it had never occurred to me that, in her own way, she might be as isolated in the cul-de-sac as I was.

For a while things were rough for her, and she put on what looked like thirty pounds overnight. I tried to keep an open door for her whenever she came around to unburden herself over a cup of coffee. It took nearly two years for her to get her life together again and relaunch her career, but she finally found a job in Minneapolis and put her house on the market. Before she left she had a farewell party for neighbors, friends, even her ex-husband. She invited me and I was glad I was between trips abroad and able to attend.

Now that Gwen has moved away, there is no one among the neighbors with whom I exchange more than casual remarks about the weather or the odd recommendation for handymen and house painters. Ironic, isn't it, that now that Gwen is gone, I am the resident with the longest seniority in the cul-de-sac?

SAMIA SERAGELDIN is the author of three books: *The Cairo House*, about growing up in Egypt; *The Naqib's Daughter*; and *Love Is Like Water and Other Stories*, which is partly set in Chapel Hill, where she has made her home for more than twenty years. She has published essays on Islam, women, Arab American writing, and counterterrorism.

A Life of Cooking

(A selection from *Mama Dip's Kitchen*)

MILDRED COUNCIL

I WAS BORN A COLORED BABY GIRL in Chatham County, North
Carolina, to Ed Cotten and Effie Edwards Cotten; grew up a Negro in
my youth; lived my adult life black; and am now an eighty-two-year-old
American. I have always known myself as Mildred Edna Cotten Council.
The cultural names haven't changed my feelings of being an American
citizen. I have experienced the Negro or black American cultural world in
a tiny area of the United States of America. I grew up and lived in poverty
most of my life without knowing it. My children, too, grew up in poverty
never knowing that they were poor. Our house just leaked. No screen
doors. An outdoor bathroom and little money. . . .

I was raised on a farm in . . . Chatham County, where I started
cooking at an early age. Before that, I could only pretend to cook and feed
the dolls that I made out of bottles and wood moss with cornsilk for their
long hair. . . . I would feed them mud pies. Many years later, I changed
the mud pie recipe to edible ingredients and created a new dessert for my
restaurant. The coconut and nuts always remind me of the small rocks

and sticks that would be in the dirt mixed with water that I served to my cornsilk dolls. . . .

One morning in about 1938, when I would have been around nine, Papa said the words that made me so happy. As our whole family started out to the field that morning after breakfast for the plowing and planting, he looked at me and said, "You stay here and fix a little something to eat." When Papa said the wonderful words to me, I had already been dreaming about cooking. . . .

I was called *Dip* by my brothers and sisters from an early age because I was so tall (today, I'm six feet, one inch) and had such long arms that I could reach way down in the rain barrel to scoop up a big dipperful of water when the level was low. Filling up water buckets for the kitchen had its benefits, though, as it was on my trips in and out of the kitchen with water that I first learned to cook, watching how . . . my older sisters and friends made things with their *dump cooking.* . . .

Dump cooking means no recipes, just measure by eye and feel and taste and testing. Cooking by feel and taste has been a heritage among black American women since slavery, and that's the way I learned to cook. When I talk about dump cooking I am thinking of fresh vegetables (planting and tending a vegetable patch and then cooking and canning its products have also been traditions for black women), homegrown or from a farmers' market. I think of peeling potatoes, stringing beans, chopping onions, hulling peas, washing greens, and more. Farm fresh is the highlight of country dump cooking. If you buy food too far ahead, it's not fresh when you cook it. . . .

The work was hard, but we were always a happy family. I don't think Papa wanted us to see the pain that people talked about later in growing up. He was our assurance, and he dedicated his life to his seven children, as well as several other children, during and after the Depression. [My mother had died when I was a baby.] I guess he didn't want to think about how much better life would have been if Mama had lived. She had gone to Bennett College and was a teacher at Baldwin School. . . .

When food was short, we had fun just seeing each other spread food all over the plate so it looked like a lot and counting how many biscuits each of us ate. If the butter gave out before it got to you, you had to sop your biscuits with side meat or put shoulder grease in your molasses and sop your biscuits in that. . . .

The second Sunday in August was the time for one of my favorite occasions—the homecoming feast at Hamlet Chapel Colored Methodist Episcopal Church. . . . The women dressed so gracefully with their handmade broomstick shirtwaist dresses covered by starched and ironed feed-sack aprons to keep their dresses clean. Their hair would be shining with grease and rolled up with hairpins, with a straw hat pressing on their forehead. They served dinner on a long wooden table nailed between two cedar trees near the church well and laughed and chattered as they spread fried chicken and vegetables of every kind on the table, cutting up pies and cakes to feed an army of hungry men, women, and children. This was a great time in between plowing, hoeing, and picking, and I longed to be able to cook good things for people to eat from my earliest memories. . . .

We had all started at Baldwin School, a one-room school built of planks that had never been painted. The potbellied stove, with its long pipe through the ceiling and roof, stood almost in the middle of the room, near the teacher's desk. One teacher taught all grades. We all studied, ate lunch, and got out of school at the same time. . . .

When my sister Myrtle—we always called her *Big*—got very sick and was put in a plaster body cast after an eighteen-month stay at Duke Hospital, we all had to take turns going to school so somebody could stay with her. Infantile paralysis, or polio as it was later called, kept her in a cast for two years until it was removed and she could learn to walk again. Whoever went to school brought the lessons home for the others, so we all kept learning, including Big. The same thing would happen when harvest time came and family members or neighbors had to stay out of school to help with the crops. . . .

When Baldwin School closed, my family moved . . . down the road to be on the bus route to Pittsboro's Horton High School. The farm was much smaller, but Papa said the soil was better, and, most important, the land-lord wanted only a quarter of the harvest. . . . On the new farm we grew watermelons, cantaloupes, peas, and lima beans, which we sold to the Creel Store on Franklin Street in Chapel Hill. I started washing and ironing for the new landlord, though I was still cooking and canning for the family, as well as helping with the plowing and the planting. I loved to plow the field until the planes started zooming so low overhead after World War II started.

We worked the new farm for two years, but after Papa sold the timber on his family's homeplace, we moved back to Papa's home farm . . . World War II took two of my older brothers into the service. By then, tobacco had become the crop to grow. But the first year we planted tobacco the govern-ment came and cut down two long rows because Papa had gone over his allotment.

Soon after that harvest, in 1945, Papa bought a house in Chapel Hill. . . . When [he] made up his mind that we would move there, I was really upset. I had been to town with him before [and had] seen girls in bobby socks, pleated skirts, and sweaters, with shiny combs and magno-lias in their hair, and I just couldn't see myself sitting in a classroom with them. . . . Papa moved us into town in a one-horse wagon. When I saw the movie *The Color Purple*, it reminded me of our move from Chatham County into Chapel Hill. . . .

In late 1945, I met Joe Council, fresh from the army. When he took me home to meet his mother, I found her a very likable person who cooked like me. With her fur coat, turkey- or peacock-feathered, wide-brim hats, and high-heel shoes, she made me feel something I had never experienced before, especially in the way she talked to her son as if they were the best of friends. She made me realize what it felt like to have a mother around. I could talk to her like I thought I would have been able to talk to my own mother, if she had lived. . . . I began to teach Miss Mary, as I called Joe's mother, to spell and write her name because Joe and I needed her to sign for us so we could get married. Even though Joe was not my sisters' choice for me because they thought he was too old, we were married in 1947.

We stayed with Miss Mary after we were married, until a cooking disaster sent me home to Papa. No matter what I did in Miss Mary's pans, I could never make brown gravy to go over the hamburger patties for supper; it was always gray, and Miss Mary was very unhappy about that. So I went home. Many tears and several days later, Joe came to stay in my family's house with Papa, too.

Times were very hard after the war for everyone. Joe worked at the sawmill, like a lot of other men, but when it rained there was no work and no money. I began work in the dining hall on the University of North Carolina campus, preparing vegetables for the cooks, and as a short-order cook in the Carolina Coffee Shop, which is now one of the few restaurants in Chapel Hill that is older than mine.

When I began having my babies — our first child, Norma, was born in 1949 — I could work only until they found out I was pregnant. Between then and 1957, all my other seven children (including twins in 1953) were born in between different jobs. The hardest time in my life was after the twins' birth, because both of them — and I — became sick. For almost a year, my right eye would not close, and people began to call me *Mrs. Boe,* for the man with a patch over his eye on the Bohemian Beer label.

My cooking continued — at Kappa Sigma fraternity and at St. Anthony Hall, when Charles Kuralt was a student and lived there, and for Roland Giduz and his family. Joe's parents opened Bill's Bar-B-Q [also called the Chicken Box] on Graham Street. It was a landmark during the integration era because it served lunches for jailed demonstrators. I worked there, too.

My first job doing family cooking was for a Mrs. Patterson. (All I ever knew her as was "Mrs. Patterson"; at that time, blacks used only the last names of their employers.) Her family drank fresh orange juice every morning for breakfast, and I would take the peels home to dry so we could chew on them in bad weather to sweeten bad breath. Now I know they probably helped ward off colds, but I didn't know that then. I still keep some over a warm place on the stove.

One day Mrs. Patterson told me to cook some sweet potatoes. She didn't say they were for a pie for dessert, but I just assumed that they were and boiled them. I guessed wrong, however, as she wanted them for the main dinner (though I never knew exactly how she wanted them cooked). When I realized my mistake, I decided to try something—I was never given recipes or a cookbook on my cooking jobs—so I mashed them and then put butter, Karo syrup, canned milk, orange juice, a handful of sugar, and a pinch of salt in them. The thought came to me to squeeze the oranges and put the potato mixture in the orange peel cups, then bake them.

At suppertime, I set the table and put the food on, but I was so afraid of what I had done with the sweet potatoes that as they sat down I went to stand at the swinging door to hear if I was going to get fired. But what I heard them say was that the potatoes were *soooo* good. My heart said, *Yes, yes, yes, Dip.* And I've been making up my own recipes and cooking them ever since.

In 1976, I was working at NC Memorial Hospital when George Tate, who was the first black realtor in town, offered me the opportunity to take over a failing restaurant on Rosemary Street. I didn't even have the money to put anything down on the deal until my next paycheck. I had only $64 to buy enough food from a local grocer to make breakfast the first day that my restaurant opened. On a Saturday evening, around seven o'clock, some of my children and I went in and cleaned nearly all night getting ready for our first day.

Sunday morning I stopped by Fowler's Food Store on Franklin Street to shop for breakfast. I purchased bacon, sausage, eggs, grits, flour, coffee, sugar, salt, catsup, chickens, Crisco, cheese, cornmeal, and trash bags, spending almost all of my money and not realizing that I could not have changed a ten dollar bill if someone had given me one first thing that morning. I don't know how many times we ran out of eggs and bacon. The breakfast trade was good enough that I left for the grocery store to buy food to make lunch, and then I used the money from lunch to buy food for the evening dinner. At the end of the day, my profit counted out to $135, and I was in business! I named my restaurant Dip's Country Kitchen.

Monday was a rather busy day for me — back to Fowler's to purchase Coca-Colas; then back to the restaurant to make pies; then to Durham to apply for a restaurant license.

I went from eighteen to twenty-two seats in the restaurant in a year. Not able to add any more seats, we began a take-out business. By 1985, I was able to rent the space adjoining my restaurant and remodeled to seat ninety. Soon the restaurant was equipped with a walk-in refrigerator, two ovens, two steam tables, two fryers, and a dish-washing machine. . . .

Since then, I have not looked back. The name of the restaurant changed — to just Dip's — after a trademark challenge. I've taken business management courses at UNC and several seminars to improve my management skills. And I've been able to hire several of my children and grandchildren, plus nieces and nephews, to work in the restaurant over the years. In 1998 I purchased the land across the street from the leased property where I had been in business since 1976 and built my own restaurant, which opened early in 1999 — with the name Mama Dip's Kitchen — and will be a legacy to my children.

The restaurant menu has changed with the times. We now offer vegetable platters, for example. However, there are still people in the community who are interested in cooking game meat, like rabbit and squirrel. Recently, someone called the restaurant and said that he had caught a raccoon in his garbage can and wanted to know how to cook it.

Preparing and eating different foods has been a mind and soul experience for me. Over the years I have observed that many important discussions take place and many important decisions get made at a table over a plate of food. All over the world, each country has its own cuisine, and whatever the agenda, food is always important. Whether it's at a picnic or a fancy dinner, food always brings joy to family, friends, and strangers. The best is sometimes the easiest to make. Southern cooking seems the simplest.

. . . Years ago, people started asking me to write a cookbook. It was a complicated and time-consuming process—mostly because what I've done all my life is dump cooking. . . . With that in mind, I tell people to modify and adapt the recipes as they like. Experiment with them. Don't worry if your brown sugar is dark or light, if your mustard is yellow or Dijon. Use what you have. Try it different ways. Use your imagination. Treat the recipes like sewing patterns—stretch or alter them to fit.

Sharing my cooking with the community reminds me of bringing my dolls together so many years ago for some old-fashioned mud pies. It's another thing in my life that I can be thankful for—spreading my love and happiness like pumpkin seeds all around.

MILDRED "MAMA DIP" COUNCIL is the author of two cookbooks, *Mama Dip's Kitchen* (from which this essay is adapted) and *Mama Dip's Family Cookbook*. The owner of Mama Dip's Kitchen, she has appeared on the Food Network and "Good Morning America."

The Beauty Queen of Chapel Hill

MORETON NEAL

"SHE LOOKED JUST LIKE THAT, a month ago," my husband commented when he saw the image. The occasion was the memorial service of Georgia Carroll Kyser in Gerrard Hall. There she was, beaming down on us from a white screen, majestic in evening wear and pearls, as gorgeous as any mature woman had a right to look. Her warm, self-possessed smile showed an old pro's comfort in front of a camera as well as a human connection with the photographer, and thereby everyone who saw the picture—in this case, a packed house of family, friends, and admirers who came to mourn her passing at age ninety-one.

"I'm ready for my close-up," she seemed to say. "Remember me like this" . . . as if she thought she might one day lose her looks. That never happened.

The power of the photograph was not a surprise to any of us. After all, Georgia Carroll had been a famous cover girl in her heyday just before the Second World War. "The most beautiful girl in the world," she was called in a *Redbook* article, circa 1939. Steichen, Horst, and other renowned photographers of the era had photographed her flawless face back then. But this particular photo had been taken when Georgia was in her late sixties. Her rare beauty remained intact. Would Grace Kelly have looked so good had she lived to be sixty-five?

The moment Georgia and her famous husband, bandleader Kay Kyser, set foot in Chapel Hill, our bastion of academia became a glamorous place to live.

The Kysers hadn't been married long when they moved here in 1950. They'd met when she was twenty-one and had been acting in Hollywood for a few years. Kay's star had risen even higher from his leading roles in a series of popular movies at that time. Georgia, too, proved successful enough on the silver screen to buy and decorate her own home in Beverly Hills.

When Kay's Kollege of Musical Knowledge went on tour to entertain the troops in World War II, Georgia Carroll signed on as the band's lead female singer. The nubile starlet made quite an impression on the older bandleader, and just as life sometimes does imitate art, he fell in love with her. On the spur of the moment, the couple eloped when the band, conveniently, played Las Vegas. So often the ethereal bride wearing haute-couture wedding gowns in the pages of *Vogue*, Georgia liked to poke fun at herself: At her own nuptials, she wore a "rump-sprung" black suit.

After a blissful half decade as a Beverly Hills wife and mother, Georgia suddenly found herself in a small Southern university town. Kay, at the pinnacle of his media popularity, had left show biz to become a Christian Science practitioner, envisioning a quiet, meaningful life in the village where he had graduated from college. Blindsided, his young wife faced a radically different lifestyle from that to which she had become accustomed—socializing with the families of Kay's pals, Bob Hope, Bing Crosby, and Edgar Bergen. Now here she was, two small daughters in tow and another soon to come, moving into the broken-down old Hooper-Howell House on Franklin Street bequeathed to Kay by his bachelor uncle, Professor Vernon Howell.

Georgia took the bull by the horns (to use one of her favorite expressions) and immersed herself in local culture, and in the process, became enchanted with the charming historic village. She studied the area's architectural vernacular before renovating their early nineteenth-century house, careful to preserve its historic character. She roamed the Carolina countryside for yet-to-be-trendy primitive antiques at a time when most town folk sat on either Danish modern chairs or Victorian settees. Using her keen eye and skills picked up from movie set designers, along with an insider's acquaintance with the loveliest of Beverly Hills domiciles, she turned Uncle Vernon's house into a cozy showplace, soon to become a popular gathering spot for neighbors and visitors. Her house, as had her face years before, appeared in national magazines.

Her love affair with the Hooper-Howell House led to a passion for historic preservation, resulting in the creation (with Ida Friday) of the Chapel Hill Preservation Society. Her design skills, honed during the process, were sought after, and she generously helped friends transform their own homes. The Horace Williams House, home of the preservation society, was lovingly and authentically decorated by Georgia. Public spaces including the UNC president's house and the Carolina Inn dining room benefited from her touch. The beauty queen had become an alchemist, transmuting ordinary rooms into spectacular ones, as if by magic.

As her children grew up, Georgia began to take classes at UNC. It was in one of those classes that she first met Ida Friday, the young wife of Bill Friday who would soon become the university's president and the Kysers' Franklin Street neighbor. Thus began two important relationships for Georgia, a close friendship with the Friday family and an abiding commitment to higher education. When she graduated in 1971 with a BA in fine arts, the Fridays honored her with a party at the president's house with three chancellors in attendance. Kay proudly presented his wife with a homemade document giving Georgia Kyser, a "PhD in MFD — Mighty Fine Doings."

A liberal arts education opened Georgia's mind to new ideas, and she began to take the family to Europe every summer instead of visiting their old show business cronies in Beverly Hills. "The more I learned about art and art history, the more attracted I was to Europe," she said. "I wanted to see the museums, paintings, the old buildings . . . gradually California seemed farther away and Europe became closer."

From her travels, she brought back an interest in French cooking (Julia Child had yet to appear on our TV screens), unusual antiques and artifacts, and Mediterranean tableware before it became fashionable — all used to entertain her wide circle of friends. Georgia was also a collector of people and enjoyed putting together academics, artists, local trade-folk, and North Carolina blue bloods. As a result of her social matchmaking, her parties were lively and energizing. "The great thing about Chapel Hill is that there is no reigning social strata here," she truly believed, oblivious to the prestige she brought to the community. Ironically, her appearance at any gathering automatically made it an A-list event. Long after Kay passed away, Queen Georgia was courted by organizations to amp up the glamour factor at their fundraisers. She never failed to light up a room.

If Georgia's beauty had been just skin-deep, we wouldn't feel her loss so profoundly. We loved her because of her generous heart. She took people under her expansive wings — all kinds of people — from the show-biz friends who dropped in from Hollywood to the foreign students who boarded in her basement. When my first husband, Bill Neal, and I moved Restaurant La Residence from Fearrington to Rosemary Street, she invited us (with our two small children) to stay at her house until we finished the renovation. She helped decorate the new venue, even volunteering to put up wallpaper and paint trim. Georgia may have appeared to be a queen bee, but she could get down and work with the drones to create beauty, her passion in life.

Like her interior decorator friend, Sister Parish, Georgia had the visual equivalent of perfect pitch. She was hypersensitive to anything off-key in her field of vision; her natural thoroughness drove her never to accept anything most mortals would call "just fine." I dare say, the word *fine* was not in Georgia's vocabulary—just ask her upholsterer, paint mixer, or gardener. And Lord help her hairdresser! From her time behind the scenes in Hollywood, Georgia knew that beauty had a lot to do with illusion, and creating that illusion was hard work. She was willing to go the distance. This was one of the lessons I learned from Georgia—how far to go and when to stop.

The most remarkable and irreplaceable quality about Georgia was her aura. It encompassed everyone around her. She had a make-believe quality, undamaged by the disappointments and the losses that came from outliving her husband, many of her friends, and her daughter, Carroll. In Georgia's presence, food tasted better, music sounded more vibrant, conversation was livelier than anywhere else. Her world, even toward the end, was a beautiful place. Around her, we even seemed to look better than we usually did. Of course, one made an effort to spruce up just to please her. She disdained sloppy clothes, once revealing that she had never worn a pair of blue jeans in her life.

A month before she died, Georgia was the guest of honor at a Christmas gathering given by her old friends, Ann Stewart and Randall Roden. Though the event took place at the Cedars Retirement Community clubhouse instead of the Hooper-Howell House, Ann and Randall tried to recreate the Kysers' annual carol-sing, complete with her old neighbor, Bill Irvine, at the piano and sheet music (to help us remember every single verse, as Georgia preferred). For more than a half hour, we sang without her, all sharing the same worry: Perhaps she was too frail to make it. But suddenly there she was. All eyes turned to take her in—coiffed, bejeweled, and dazzling in a green satin jacket. She always knew how to make an entrance. Even in a wheelchair, an oxygen tube in her nose, Georgia was the most beautiful woman there. As always, she lit up the room and the party began.

MORETON NEAL is an interior designer and food writer. The author of *Remembering Bill Neal: Favorite Recipes from a Life in Cooking* and *Chapel Hill Food Lover's Guide*, she is food editor of and a regular columnist for *Metro Magazine*. For fifteen years, she was co-host of "Food Forum" and "The Better Living Show" on WDNC Radio.

Down among the Bones, the Darks, the Sparrows

JIM SEAY

THERE ARE THE BOONES TOO, maybe kin to the Bones, and the Lloyds, the Merritts, the Rigsbees. Old Carrboro families my son is among in the under-earth. When I can free myself of the grief of his death, eight years ago, it amuses me to think of my Josh entering that dominion, him strange to them in his ways and from unfamiliar family, not of their place. But with a sweetness and bravery and wry smile those folks could not long fail to accept and allow into their fold.

At the moment, a bee is testing a plastic flower at the base of Josh's gravestone, then it moves on to the asters, marigolds, Russian sage, and rosemary I have brought to his grave today. The honey to be made of the dead, the blent nectar gathered among the flowers for the Bones, the Boones, Vonnie and Annie Horton, Darian Earl Bryan dead in a car wreck at thirty-nine, his oval portrait in porcelain, the Darks, the Sparrows.

Camber is that subtle, slight rise of an arch in favor of support for what is above it. The man who was the project manager for the building of my house pointed it out to me before the sheet-rockers covered it. Camber. Laminated beams, cambered and bearing the weight of my bed above. You can see it on I–40, whatever is your interstate. Tractor-trailers, eighteen-wheelers, long open trailers cambered most freely when they are dead-heading, bound for home with no load. Free-bedded. The camber there like a waiting angel. At an angle from Josh's grave is the Woodcock/ Camber grave. I don't know the family, Woodcocks, Cambers, but Josh is among them. One of the truths of fatherhood, not knowing how balanced is a son's full weight in the world, or, in Josh's case, how his illness lay on the given camber.

When freed from the straitjacket he wore home early from music camp one summer, he went straight to fluent, graceful tai chi and years of every wrong medicine we could offer. Then one that gave him years of clarity and whimsy and a manner all his own. And finally weight his heart couldn't bear. Enlarged, it stopped in his sleep at age thirty-three.

Josh is buried at the end of a row of graves running parallel to the backmost road of Westwood Cemetery. His mother, Lee, and I shared the duties of putting him to rest. She asked if I would find a burial plot for his ashes. The cost of a plot in the Old Chapel Hill Cemetery, even if one could find a family willing to sell a space there, was beyond reason. I went to the town hall in Carrboro, the adjacent town where Josh once lived and where he worked in Lee's sushi restaurant, and I found that there were available plots in Westwood. On the map there was a space, serendipity, at the end of the row parallel to the back road. And it turned out to be beneath a tree.

That is where my dog, Neville, and I are today. Neville, a she, goes straight for the October pumpkin next to the flowers I've placed at Josh's grave. Sniff, sniff. And then on to other graves. Bones, Darks, Sparrows. My guess is that Lee has left the pumpkin, along with flowers of her own.

I empty the rainwater from the little plastic music-box piano that was left on Josh's gravestone shortly after his burial. It is a small-scale grand and has a profile of Elvis on the top. It used to play "Love Me Tender" when wound up. After a few rains it could barely plink out Elvis's plea, and then it gave up. But it's still there in its mysterious provenance. When I first found the piano, I called Lee to see if she put it there, but she said no, she thought I had. To this day, we have no idea who beyond family summoned our son's love. And counted on that summons being heard. Two graves down, on the Butterfield grave, someone has left a scale model Corvette, top down, headed east toward Josh. Maybe the Butterfield boy is taking Josh for a ride. I don't know. As Marlon, probably aware of St. Peter's similar question, asked his lover in *Last Tango*, "Quo vadis, baby?"

JIM SEAY has published four collections of poems, most recently *Open Field, Understory*. His essays have appeared in many publications including *Esquire* and *Antaeus*. He teaches English and creative writing at the University of North Carolina at Chapel Hill.

Street Scenes 🦎

The Cocineros of Franklin Street

PAUL CUADROS

WALKING INTO SUTTON'S DRUG STORE on Franklin Street has always been a little like stepping back in time. But today walking through the aisles of over-the-counter cold remedies, magazines, bottles of soft drinks, passing by the formica tables and booths is also a little like stepping into a different part of the world where North Carolina drawls spoken around the lunch counter swirl with clipped staccato Spanish.

Marta moves behind the counter with ease and quickness. You need to be light on your feet behind the counter at Sutton's and nimble in front of the griddle and food prep station. Dressed in a simple Sutton's white T-shirt and jeans, Marta greets me with a simple, "*Hola*," knowing right away I speak Spanish. But many people who stand behind the counter and who sit down at it today do, too. Even some of the old-timers, and there are a lot of those at Sutton's, have picked up a word or two to talk to the staff.

"*Ya esta listo los pancaques,*" Marta says to Dimas, the grillman. Communication behind the counter is swift and precise as the patrons' orders come in. Dimas, a short but hefty young man in his twenties, takes a red ketchup squirt bottle and squeezes some oil on the griddle. He pours pancake batter.

The morning breakfast rush is easing up a bit. There is a break in the action for some conversation and play. Marta switches from Spanish to English easily depending on whom she is talking to. Between the workers behind the counter it is Spanish. *"Ya viene los chicos y las chicas,"* she says to Dimas, giving him a heads-up that the students are on their way in and sitting down at the booths up front. Marta is originally from Puebla, Mexico, a small, poor town located in the center east of the country. Dimas is from Honduras originally and has been living in the U.S. for the past ten years.

Up and down Franklin Street the *cocineros y cocineras,* the cooks of some of Franklin Street's traditional and established restaurants, are from south of the border. Just down the block from Sutton's, Ye Olde Waffle Shoppe's griddle is manned by Latino cooks. Many of these workers are virtually invisible as they chop, pour, scramble, and serve up food along Chapel Hill's main strip. But at Sutton's they are front and center—a blended shake or *liquado* of vanilla and tamarindo.

The breakfast patrons today are a mix of Latino workers, pausing for a quick breakfast sandwich before heading off to the construction site, professors, judges, and students from all ethnicities, the red-blood cells that course through the city's heart.

A Latino man sits down at the counter one seat over from me and greets Marta, *"Hola, listo para trabajar,"* he says ordering coffee. "Hello. Ready to start the work day." A black student leans over his paper and tries his Spanish on the worker. They exchange *"Buenos dias"* and talk about the good food.

Dimas has spent the morning grilling and hanging up new photos of Carolina's athletic teams that cover the walls like wallpaper. The Latino man at the counter complains to Marta about how hard the work situation has been in the Triangle. Marta tells him he needs to be optimistic. "You have to have a positive view of life or else your health will fail," she says to him. He listens but shakes his head.

Dimas returns to the griddle. To watch Dimas work behind the counter is to see an artist, painting on a canvas griddle with vegetable oil, eggs, cheese, bacon, and fire—he is in his element, knows his station, and has the items stored in his memory. He could fill an order with his apron over his head.

There is a routine. What may seem to be random moves are deft turns and spins equal to some of the ball players on the wall. A squeeze from the red bottle goes into the silver and black skillet in a circular motion, an egg is broken in a flash in a white bowl, the shell thrown quickly away with a flick of the wrist. Dimas has broken a lot of eggs. There is no mess with Dimas's eggs and no shell pieces in the white bowl as he violently gives the whites and yolks a swirl with a simple fork. Then a pour into the skillet and an adjustment of the fire. Dimas's words move as fast as he does. He's a shootist with a joke and likes to tease the señoras who work behind the counter with him.

"*Vamos a bailar esta viernes,*" he says to them with a flash of his big eyes, asking them to come dancing with him on Friday. He tells them he's going to be taking a very pretty young girl to the dance. Marta looks at him sideways and asks him if his wife is coming, too. He laughs and says of course not. She'll be home. They laugh and ask him if all Hondurans treat their wives this way.

Dimas sticks his hands into a large brown cardboard box and pulls out a sheet of bacon the size of a desk calendar and slaps it on the griddle. The bacon immediately begins to bubble and crack. Dimas needs to keep up with the bacon and have plenty on hand for the sandwich orders that come in. It's all in Dimas's head, how to stay ahead of the hungry pack.

"Moo-cho-Dee-ner-row!" says the elderly man in the brown fedora as he sits down at the counter. Marta responds, "*Buenos dias!*" Again, "Moo-cho-Dee-ner-row!" the man says, slapping a plastic bottle of maple syrup on the counter. It's sugar-free. He's diabetic. Dimas responds, "*Si, mucho dinero,* one day."

"I need a pancake like this," says the man making a circle in the air. "A circular pancake." Marta asks him what is he drinking. "Ah-goo-wah."

Dimas shoves the cooked bacon to the side and scrapes the griddle clean. Then he begins to pour seven pancakes from the plastic container with batter and carefully place them on the griddle, making sure he has good separation between the meat and the cakes.

Henry, an older black man, sits down with his paper and says, "*Buenos dias*, Dimas." Dimas smiles and says, "Henri, do you want coffee? Milk? Or a woman?" Henry laughs. "*Quiero chocolate caliente*," he says with a thick English accent but perfect Spanish.

"Okay," Dimas says. Marta hands him a green and white ticket, an order for a bacon-egg-and-cheese sandwich on wheat bread. "Okay, *ya esta listo*," he says, pulling some bacon from a stack already cooked. "It's ready."

PAUL CUADROS is an award-winning investigative reporter who is an assistant professor at the School of Journalism at the University of North Carolina at Chapel Hill. His work appears in many publications, including *Time Magazine* and the *Chapel Hill News*. He is the author of *A Home on the Field: How One Championship Soccer Team Inspires Hope for the Revival of Small Town America.*

Watch

ALAN SHAPIRO

Bad luck, bad history:
The right arm shriveled,
the hand curled
in on itself,
unusable,
the crippled gait

I try hard
not to stare at
when I see him
in the playground
I walk past
every day,

out on the court
alone, his good hand
hoisting the ball
up, banging the ball
on rim or backboard
so that it bounds

away and he has to
lumber after,
the gimped leg dragged
like a ball and chain
across the blacktop
over and over,

indefatigable,
his voice announcing
the last seconds
of the game forever
playing in his head
that he's always winning.

Genetic damage.
Damage of history,
of shame inside
the pleasure inside
the pity of
not being him,

of being white,
and then the panic
the day he calls me over,
saying, Hey man
can you help
a brother out?

Panic of borders
breached, of history
in the sour air
I'm breathing as I reach
into my pocket
for what he wants,

sour air of history
when he sighs,
and shakes his head,
and smiles at me
so wearily
without surprise

as if his days were
days of just
this kind of thing
to get through, to
put up with, saying,
shit man, I don't

want your money,
holding out to me
the wristwatch
he can't with one
hand, understand?
buckle to his wrist,

and could I do it?
and now I'm fumbling
with the frayed band
that I can't make
fit through the opening
of the metal clasp,

and so he talks me
through it, teaching
me how, the way
a father does,
teaching the child
something he better

learn, teaching it
patiently but
with a patience that
the tone says
isn't inexhaustible,
You got to slow

down, just ease it
through the slot
a little softer
like it wants
to go there on
its own, like that,

man, yeah, like that,
and it's done,
he's turned away,
he's finished with my
being anyone
of use, I'm finished

being useful,
and again the cocked
arm hurls the ball
up toward the hoop
and the fans go crazy
as the announcer
cries out three two one.

ALAN SHAPIRO is the author of ten books of poetry, two memoirs, and the novel, *Broadway Baby.* He is the recipient of numerous awards and is a member of the American Academy of Arts and Sciences. He is a professor of English and Creative Writing at the University of North Carolina at Chapel Hill.

Where the Parking Lot Is Now

SY SAFRANSKY

IT WAS MY FIRST OFFICE, a narrow, second-story dormer room with barely enough space for a desk and a chair. I didn't spend much time there. During the summer I avoided it because of the heat. By the following winter I'd moved across the street. Still, that small room was important to me. It gave legitimacy (in my mind, anyway) to my pennilessness and restlessness and to my quixotic dream of starting a magazine.

A bookstore occupied the first floor of the ramshackle, two-story house. If you lived in Chapel Hill in the Seventies, it might have occupied a place in your imagination, too.

People rarely went to the Community Bookstore merely to buy a book. They went there to run into friends, to check the bulletin board for a ride or a roommate, to sit on the front stoop and read. The building was tucked away in a shabby neighborhood where rents were low; they had to be for an alternative business to survive. Though progressive by Southern standards, Chapel Hill was still something of a cultural backwater in 1974: Ideas took root more slowly; the transcendental promise of certain philosophies (and certain drugs) was whispered, not shouted.

Richard, the owner, didn't keep regular hours. The store opened when he showed up. Sometimes I'd find him outside, his long blond hair pulled back as he trimmed the bushes or practiced juggling or chatted with regulars.

Inside there were books everywhere: books stacked on chairs, books stacked on tables, tall crooked stacks of books in the hall. The architecture of our thinking back then was no less imposing or precarious. As a generation we were having a love affair with truth, a lover we'd betray again and again. The Sixties were receding into myth. Books about starting a commune or surviving a bad acid trip were being marketed as hippie memorabilia. Hucksters already had a stranglehold on America's spiritual renaissance: For every slender tract by someone sincerely yearning to know God there would soon be a hundred fat mass-market paperbacks, each more hokey than the last.

But for those of us still struggling to redefine ourselves and the culture, the spirit of the Sixties lived on; it was the spirit of change, after all. The bookstore was a place where we could share our discoveries and our naiveté, read and talk and talk some more, like gold panners sifting for a few pure nuggets. The back-to-the-land movement, antinuclear marches, civil-rights protests, psychedelics, Eastern mysticism, natural foods, feminism, environmentalism — we knew these were connected somehow, and not just by a *Woodstock* soundtrack. Something had changed; like blind people touching different parts of an elephant, we couldn't agree what it was, only that it was big.

In addition to books, Richard carried health foods and an odd assortment of products: hammocks, bowls and cleavers from China, cast-iron pots and pans, drawstring pants. Some items sat on the shelf for years, but Richard didn't seem to mind. No ordinary businessman, he might ask a customer to wait so that he could finish preparing lunch for himself in his small kitchen. Then again, he might let his steaming bowl of rice and vegetables grow cold while he helped someone else. I never saw him rush.

Nor did Richard go out of his way to make the store inviting. The building was cold in the winter, hot in the summer. There were no chairs placed at strategic angles to encourage conversation. There was no cappuccino bar. Yet the store was part of the social glue of the community, a place where newcomers could meet those who had lived in town for years; where people who thought alike—or thought they thought alike—could fall in love with new ideas and, occasionally, with each other.

A glowing stick of incense perched near the cash register, the smell of fresh new books waiting to be shelved, and the sour leftovers in Richard's kitchen all gave the musty building its unique fragrance, just as the extravagant dreams of those who walked through the door helped give the era its unique shape.

Before renting the dormer room upstairs from the bookstore, I'd gotten by without an office. I worked on *The Sun* at my kitchen table or in my favorite booth at the coffee shop. Eventually, though, I wanted a place in town where I could meet with writers and store back issues. I rented the room for $25 a month.

I was right about the back issues. Boxes of unsold magazines soon lined the wall. Visitors, however, were rare. I'd sit alone in that small room, staring out the window, wondering if the world really needed another magazine. Before moving to Chapel Hill, I'd quit a well-paying newspaper job, vowing to starve rather than compromise my beliefs. It was a defining moment. I've never regretted it. But the problem with defining moments is that they don't last. The lights fade, the curtain falls, and you walk off the stage and out the door into the same narrow alley, past the same barking dog. Everything has changed and nothing has changed. Back in your little apartment (still little), the dishes still need to be washed, the bills still need to be paid, and your wobbly beliefs still need to be tested day after day— with no one but yourself to blame when you fail.

I failed again and again, but I didn't compromise and I didn't starve. I outgrew my cramped office, but never my affection for that narrow dormer room, where my dream didn't die.

It's odd, even in a small town like Chapel Hill, that I never moved my office more than a block from the Community Bookstore — first, to a run-down building across the street; then, years later, to a more comfortable two-story house around the corner. From both locations, I was able to look out my window and pay homage to the past.

I continued to visit the store regularly to browse or say hello. For men who both loved words, however, Richard and I rarely had much to say to each other, as if we lived on separate peaks, unsure how to meet in the valley between us. Although we never became close friends, I enjoyed Richard's company, and I admired his style. A lanky, athletic man who wore shorts practically year-round, he loved the outdoors. He tried to live lightly on the earth, as we put it back then (before we realized how easy it was to get weighed down, and not just by possessions). He didn't believe in advertising. He didn't promote bestsellers. He never managed to shelve all the books he'd ordered before the next shipment arrived, but to him books weren't just commodities. Between picking up a book and shelving it, he might stop to read a chapter or two. In the minds of some, I suppose, Richard carried his aversion to being a businessman too far: More than once he closed the store and took a vacation the week *before* Christmas. But if the way Richard ran his business wasn't always logical, maybe that's because he'd discovered that making a living wasn't the same as making a life.

Then there was the sign. *Community Bookstore,* it read, each letter carved by hand into a rough-hewn board salvaged from an old barn.

Suspended between two tall posts, the sign was big, confident, exuberant. It looked like it would last forever. But over the years, time carved its own message into the grain. The wood grew weathered and deeply furrowed. The artfully shaped letters became hard to read.

Richard never fixed or replaced the sign, even as whole pieces of it rotted and fell away. Maybe he never liked the sign; it had been put up by the store's founder, Mike Mathers, a more gregarious and outgoing man than Richard. To me, the sign looked rustic and handsome, but to Richard it might have looked like a billboard. Perhaps he had faith that new customers would find the store on their own. Of course, with each passing year, fewer and fewer did.

Characteristically, when Richard was ready to move on, he didn't announce a going-out-of-business sale. He just stopped showing up. The sloping lot became overgrown with weeds. Vines started climbing up the walls and through the windows. One day, I heard the building was going to be torn down; a nearby church wanted the land for a parking lot. The sign was pretty much gone by then; only the curved cedar posts remained.

Time, that joker: always the same punch line.

I walked past the deserted building. It didn't look ready to die. Sure, the roof probably leaked, and a few windows were broken. But when boards are joined, they want to stay joined. How mysterious old buildings are, I thought, shaped by us and shaping us. Yet we tear them down as casually as we take out yesterday's trash.

I wondered how I'd feel when the place was gone. It would stay alive in my memory, but I couldn't take much comfort from that. Memories we're sure are indelible—how long do they really last? I can remember the way a lover's hair once smelled, but not the taste of her kisses; how long an argument lasted, but not what it was about. Even my own childhood can seem like a former lifetime, ghostly and indistinct.

I thought of my old office and my old friends, of our narcissism and our passion for change, of our willingness to take America more seriously, perhaps, than it took itself. How tempting it is today to mock the idealism of that era, or to sentimentalize it; to recall the clothes flapping on the clothesline—the patched jeans and tie-dyed shirts—but not the wind that lifted them.

Those years are gone: thousands of days compressed into a handful of images. But all eras suffer the same fate. Half of all high-school graduates don't know the difference between the Revolutionary War and the Civil War. We're dismantling the New Deal, even though the richest one percent of Americans still control one-third of the country's wealth.

I glanced up at the dormer window streaked with dirt. Years ago, I could remember the names of everyone I'd published in *The Sun*. Now there were too many names. In moments of crisis, I used to spread all the issues I'd published around me in a circle and stand at the center to ponder my next move: How would I meet my deadline? Pay the printer? Now there were so many issues there would be no place for me to stand.

When the bulldozers arrived on a crisp fall day, I walked over to the bookstore to watch. The sky was blue and beautiful with promise, but I knew better. They're tearing down an era, I thought sadly, as the bulldozers lumbered toward the store. Then I realized I was being melodramatic. They're tearing down a building, I reminded myself, not an era. The era was already gone.

The bulldozers clanged and groaned, kicking up clouds of dust. Like bullies without any imagination, they smashed the old house again and again.

SY SAFRANSKY is editor and publisher of *The Sun*, a magazine he founded in 1974. This essay was published in the April 1996 edition of *The Sun*. He is the author of *Four in the Morning*, a collection of his essays from *The Sun*. He is also editor of several anthologies, including *The Mysterious Life of the Heart: Writing from the Sun about Passion, Longing and Love* and *Paper Lanterns: More Quotations from the Back Pages of the Sun*.

In the Poetry Section of a Used Bookstore

PAUL JONES

It makes me tired just to look at them,
their weak yellowed spines, their ink soaked in.
Unreviewed and unread, even by friends,
they are anonymous and without end.

Who would pull one down, much less
pay to take one home? Poets of loneliness:
How did they see the sad verse they made?
Their hard words as stars that could not fade?

Perhaps they thought their hurt was a lamp
flame fueled by desire that will not dim
with a wick so wet, so deep, so well-trimmed,
it could glow crimson against the dusk of time.

Their passion will not heat these shelves
no matter what they gave of themselves:
What once burned bright turns quickly pale
and promising poems too soon go stale.

But somewhere others are writing more;
A seductive moon leans on their shoulders.
Is any light welcome — however poor —,
while hearts so nearly cold, still smolder?

PAUL JONES is the director of the digital library, ibiblio.org. His poetry has been published in a variety of publications, including the *News & Observer, Poetry,* and *Best American Erotic Poetry.* He is clinical associate professor of Information and Library Science and of Journalism and Mass Communication at the University of North Carolina at Chapel Hill.

Notes from the Bike Path

BILL SMITH

A PAVED BIKE PATH connects Carrboro with Chapel Hill. Since it parallels a train track rather than a street, it seems a tad wild even though it's right downtown. It is along this trail that I pick blackberries and honeysuckle flowers that I use on the summer menu at Crook's Corner. For several years now I have kept a blog that is a sort of online kitchen diary. These sketches are adapted from there.

Monday, May 12

It's less than a mile long but the bike path is an interesting bit of territory. It is the place where soccer moms with jogging strollers, the homeless, university students, and assorted drug merchants rub elbows. Generally they ignore one another, but they all seem to be interested in me and what I'm doing. There's a lot going on, our own version of Midaq Alley.

An uncommon number of botanists seem to use this path to get from the university to their apartments in Carrboro. They often stop their bikes to either question me or offer scientific tidbits. Did I know, for instance, that I am picking Japanese honeysuckle, an unwelcomed invader?

People who I would probably avoid on Franklin Street chat me up as I move up one side of the path and down the other. For a while there was a young woman who at first would talk to me in a quiet pleasant voice, asking about my tasks. Then suddenly she would be consumed by a frightening rage and begin screeching and ripping down flyers stapled to telephone poles. I haven't seen her this year.

Last summer, someone that I will refer to only as C took a particular liking to me. He would narrate as we walked, filling me in on people we passed, telling me sometimes-startling stories of life in this no-man's-land between our towns. I guess that because there is no road here, there's little supervision by the law. This is probably why I can walk up and down undisturbed, drinking beer as I pick. A large rough man, C was nice really, but years of homelessness and drug use had taken their toll. It dawned on me about mid-August that C's interest in me might be romantic in nature. I was right it turned out. When I told him I wasn't interested, he quietly gave me a kiss on the cheek and walked off. I've never seen him again either.

Thursday, May 22

Years ago on one of the Spanish-language TV channels there was a *telenovela* called "Mariana de la Noche." I never saw it but apparently its logo included a scene where Mariana swept through a flowery landscape by night. The connection was soon made in the Crook's kitchen, and I, myself, became Mariana de la Noche each evening. Modern Spanish is as changeable and adaptable as is English, so now we have a verb, *marianar. Voy a marianar* means I'm leaving to pick honeysuckle flowers and drink beer along the bike path.

The habits of honeysuckle. Different types of honeysuckle bloom at different times and have different characteristics. The first one of the season is usually a large, single, pure white blossom that prefers a bit of shade. Its blossoms pull away from the stem easily. Next comes the pink-throated variety. It has the strongest fragrance and tends to bloom in pairs of flowers that are easy to pick. Then the clustering varieties begin. These are mixed among unopened buds and leaves. At the Merritt Mill Road end of the bike trail is a particularly brittle grove of these whose vines break off when you try to harvest them. Right now all these varieties are overlapping. I've gotten very good at spotting them in dim light and at seeing them out of the corner of my eye as I whizz by on my bicycle.

Saturday, May 31

The honeysuckle is finally starting to subside, although we will probably have sorbet periodically for a while yet. The vetch, which grows with it, has died back, so now there are great snarls of dead vines around my legs as I pick. The list of characters who entertain me as I gather flowers this spring has been smaller, although there is still blackberry season to come. There is a nice lady with a West Indian accent who talks very loudly on her cell phone as she walks her dog. Once or twice she has, without warning, hung up her phone and begun talking to me the same way. No intro or anything, as if we'd been talking all along. The first time she startled me, but now I am prepared.

There was one couple that I encountered often enough this year to invite observation. They would stride purposefully down the bike trail each evening in a sort of lockstep prance. When they caught sight of me, they seemed to be reminded that there was honeysuckle for the taking, and that if they didn't hurry, I might get their portion as well as mine. They would settle in a spot just out of swatting distance where they would make exaggerated motions of picking and sucking the nectar from the flowers. They would coo to one another about the wonder of this natural serendipity. Unfortunately, they would also spit the used blossoms back into the vines causing me to avoid the spots where they had been. They were a lot more annoying than the guy who would follow me offering me a variety of drugs and prostitutes over and over again, as if he had forgotten that we had just talked a minute earlier.

Thursday, July 2

A few observations about blackberries. They take on a certain luster when they are just right. It's hard to describe, but imagine something black and translucent. Right after they pass this point, the luster dulls, but they will still be good for a day or so. They will come away in your hand without much effort. If a whole cluster is ripe, put down your pitcher or bowl and hold your open palm underneath it before you start to pick. In clusters, the berries on the bottom ripen first and the motion of picking can cause them to come off their stems and fall to the ground. When you think you have picked everything in one spot, move a few steps to the left or right, but keep your eyes on the same place. Invariably, more ripe berries will reveal themselves. June bugs love blackberries and they are dark and shiny too. Sometimes when you reach for a berry, you get a June bug instead. It's like one of those joke shop electric handshake rings.

Monday, July 6

In Spain, the word *mora* means mulberry, but in Mexico it means blackberry. This is the root of my favorite Spanish word — *morado*, meaning purple, the color of blackberries. It comes up often in pop ballads because it is the color of the bruises that love can leave on the heart. My hands have been *morado* as well lately because we are having one of the biggest blackberry seasons I can remember.

I had said that I wouldn't make blackberry pies because the wild ones had so many seeds that I was afraid they would seem gritty. However, peaches didn't show up as expected this week so I decided to make just two pies to bridge the gap. Instead of being seedy, the pies had the consistency of Fig Newtons and were perfectly delicious. It looks like we will have at least a week more of blackberry picking, so look for more pies.

Wednesday July 22

While I was picking honeysuckle in the spring, I met a guy who lived in the hut beside the junkyard. We would chat from time to time, and one of our conversations was about tomato sandwiches. It was May and we were both looking forward to them. We talked about having a tomato sandwich supper in July, but now he is gone. The little lean-to is still there, but no sign of him. I used to see him around town on his bicycle even before we met. I always notice grownups who travel exclusively by bicycle. I hope he's okay.

Thursday, July 23

The blackberries have finally given out, but it has been a generous season. It seems that I was always in too much of a hurry to savor my early evening forays and to notice the people along the trail. The same street people still prowled the bike trail, although they looked a little more flinty for another year of being homeless. They were always cordial. One guy I often saw was always somewhat wide-eyed as he contemplated the money he was saving by picking berries instead of buying them "in the shops." He would actually have beads of sweat on his upper lip and would tremble slightly as he explained his clever thriftiness.

At one point the Crook's kitchen had so much fruit from my forays along the bike path that we had blackberry pie, blackberry cobbler, and blackberries in sabayon on the menu on the same night.

There also have been a lot of wild plums this year—small yellow ones like mirabelles. They grow in a grove right beside one of my blackberry patches. We had wonderful sorbet and an even more wonderful plum curd for tarts.

BILL SMITH is the chef of Crook's Corner, one of Chapel Hill's most innovative and famous restaurants. He is the author of *Seasoned in the South*, and has been a finalist twice for the James Beard Award for Best Chef in the Southeast. He is the founder of the legendary Cat's Cradle. His blog, "A Year in the Kitchen (and on the Road)," is www.seasonedinthesouth.com/wordpress/

I Grew Up in a City

(a poem to be read aloud)

CJ SUITT of Sacrificial Poets

I grew up in a city
Where progress and distress go hand in hand
Like glove and mitt
Grew up watching egos trip
On sidewalks full of wallets and money clips
A sinking ship
Whose Captain
Reassures everyone that they should secure their *bible belts*
And stay strapped in
Director yells action
And we play
Like we don't see the props
In the form of expensive shops
And parking lots
Human rights on the chopping block
This bothers us a lot
Just not enough to tell them stop

They bulldoze blocks and hide their hands
Seemingly spontaneous construction
The way they roll these rocks and Divide the land
So fast it seems they stole the clocks and hid the sands

And on days like this
I'd like to think that there is a *plan*
Some *Framework*
That will relieve us of this same hurt
Won't leave us out in the cold and call us panhandlers when we are people
Seems there is no steeple in the *Southern Part of Heaven*
Where the Devel has made his way

                                        down

                                            . . . town
Without so much as a protestant puncture wound

We are wound in chords of sound
A cacophonous developers'
DevilOper-a
I swear I still hear Phantom forefathers
Singing Hamilton hymn in the rafters
And here in the hereafter
I wonder if history will repeat this chapter
I know faith is the substance
But it's hard not to believe what you can see

And as I start to get older
The weight of this knowledge bears heavy on my molars
Leaves me with lockjaw and sore wisdom
While my courage is clawing tooth and nail
Out of an achievement gap
A black boy from Carolina clay
Who loves sweet tea and sayin'
"Hey"
Through all of the roles we play
Whether we tear down the set
Or are simply *cast*-aways
We all simply wish
Our home were a better place to stay

CJ SUITT is founder and director of the Sacrificial Poets, a youth performance poetry organization. He facilitates intergenerational events with social justice themes, and teaches poetry workshops and educational projects at group homes for teens awaiting trial.

A Place Apart ❧

Fragrantissima

MICHAEL McFEE

AT THE NORTHEAST CORNER of Coker Arboretum—where my wife and I courted when undergraduates, where our young son later loved to roam on Sunday mornings, where I now walk en route to my campus office—is the most wonderful bush I know. Not that it's particularly exotic or rare; not that it's gorgeous to look at, though its little yellow blossoms are pleasing enough; not that you'd ever even notice it, driving by on Raleigh Street, past the stately President's House diagonally across the road. But if you're walking anywhere nearby in late February, you simply can't miss it: because *Lonicera fragrantissima* emits (as its species name rightly claims) the most fragrant of smells, sublimely fresh and sweet and evocative, neither too cloying nor too subtle, just the aroma needed to put dull winter behind us and welcome the olfactory revival of another Southern spring. Its common name, First Breath of Spring, is almost as lovely and accurate as its botanical one, because it does indeed breathe life into a new year, animating its cold clay.

To me, that bush embodies Chapel Hill, where things seem to bloom sooner and sweeter and longer than anywhere else. I don't know why that is. Maybe it's the elevation, lifting the town above the surrounding plain like some misplaced mythical mountain. Maybe it's a matter of air, a sort of atmospheric Gulf Stream that quickens the campus and the village. Or maybe, the rest of the state might say, it's those centuries of intellectual manure generated by Chapel Hill professors and students and townspeople.

Whatever. All I know is, the town's dogwoods and azaleas and other local flora are always weeks ahead of anything blooming in my yard in Durham, only seven miles away. And that's one reason I love Chapel Hill, and feel truly lucky coming here to teach or attend church or go to a restaurant or movie or ballgame: It's a place of early blooming, where plants and people can just go ahead and burst into blossom without worrying about the pressures that might hold them back elsewhere. No doubt this has its ludicrous aspects, as blooming does, but—like the arboretum itself, that botanical sanctuary, sampling the state and region and world—Chapel Hill is finally a kind of refuge, a place apart, not exactly *better* but somehow *other.* I first felt that distinctiveness in 1974, when I transferred to UNC and began to imagine myself as a writer; I still feel it now, many decades later, as a faculty member and published poet. This place is, for me, *terra fragrantissima.*

MICHAEL MCFEE'S most recent books are a chapbook of one-line poems, *The Smallest Talk*; a collection of prose, *The Napkin Manuscripts*; and a volume of poetry, *Shinemaster.* His eighth full-length collection of poems, *That Was Oasis,* will be published in 2012. He teaches in the Creative Writing Program at the University of North Carolina at Chapel Hill.

In Battle's Woods

BLAND SIMPSON

ONE OF THE FINEST OF MY FATHER'S GIFTS to me was the inborn desire to light out walking in the big woods, and one of the best given me by my mother was Chapel Hill, second of the two small Carolina towns I grew up in and one of the very few towns anywhere, of any size, that has an honest-to-God *forest* at its heart.

All my first ten years we had been coming up from down east to Chapel Hill, for her family lived here and had since the Twenties when my grandfather Page took charge of building the stadium, the bell tower, and the library up on campus. But I had never known anything of the woodlands that lay between my grandparents' big sloping slate-roof house in town on one edge of Battle Park and my aunt's and uncle's home on the other.

I can't recall who prompted me to climb up the big hill that summer of 1959 when we had just moved to Chapel Hill, but I remember hearing that I would find a castle at its peak. No one need tell a ten-year-old boy much more than that to encourage him to head for the clouds, so I entered Battle Park from the low ground east and underneath the great mountain head called Piney Prospect. I followed a twisting path that is certainly one of the same trod by General Joe Wheeler's retreating Confederate troops in April of 1865, where for a few hours they dug in at the top of this steep slope and prepared to stave off Federal cavalry, till that plan was scotched and this branch of the Southern army passed through and vacated Chapel Hill.

At the mountain top, I found a semicircular rock throne. Two boys my age, the Scott brothers, Bobby and Bill, were sitting there and, as they knew the lore and were willing to share it with me, we became immediate friends. They told me about the Gimghouls, some mysterious race of phantoms who built the small castle, with its little turreted tower and baronial hall, just up the rise from the stone seat. And they told me about Peter Dromgoole, a college student, a Virginian, killed in a misty midnight duel over a woman and thrown into one of the most fabled shallow graves in our state's history, right out in front of the castle under a rock at the center of a ring of boxwoods.

Upon the curved rock throne, facing eastward toward Raleigh thirty miles distant, was a dark bronze plaque that read:

> *In memory of Kemp Plummer Battle*
> *(1831–1919)*
> *Who Knew and Loved These Woods As No One Else*

A thousand times or more since then I have been back to that spot, always stopping to read those few words again. The Scott boys had no idea who Kemp Battle was, and for the longest time neither did I, other than that he had something to do with the university way back yonder. Much later I learned how he had ambled time and again to a large poplar in the woods to rehearse his 1849 UNC valedictory speech, and how, upon his return to Chapel Hill as the university's president when it reopened in the 1870s, he cut a path to that special tree. "The exercise was agreeable," Battle wrote in *Memories of an Old-Time Tar Heel,* adding, "This led to others until I finished the park in a rough way."

Rough was the way my friends and I liked it, and from my earliest encounter with this wilderness enclave, I was captivated. It was only fifty or sixty acres of mixed pine and hardwoods, but it seemed like 50,000; it had a rocky creek that rose just backstage of the Forest Theatre—another stone medievalism—and carved a steep valley into eastern Chapel Hill. And not knowing Kemp Battle's history ever kept me from understanding how wonderful an epitaph those sixteen words were for this man, whoever he was and whatever he had done. To me as a boy it seemed just about as good as actually being the trees and earth of the magnificent hill, having this thought set upon stone where students and townspeople would sit and ponder the verities and sometimes be able to see all the way to Raleigh and ponder that.

Battle Park was really Battle's backyard, for Senlac, his home, sits on a knoll just west of the woods. He not only carved the first trails in and about the valley, he also gave fanciful names to its features, corners, and crannies: Trysting Poplar, Anemone Spring, Fairy Vale, Lion Rock, the Triangle, Over-Stream Seat, Vale of Ione, Glen Lee, Wood-Thrush Home, Dogwood Dingle, and Flirtation Knoll. His affection for the woods was very much shared by earlier woodland ramblers than myself. Cornelia Phillips Spencer, Kemp Battle's friend and ally in reviving the university after the Civil War, for years wandered and explored Battle Park and other areas hereabouts and wrote affectionately of them as she reminisced about such natural features as the Roaring Fountain, the Meeting of the Waters, the Hunter's Spring. William Meade Prince in *The Southern Part of Heaven* said the park was "a perfect and well-balanced combination of the Garden of Eden, the Forest Primeval, and the Happy Hunting Ground," and, looking back on his turn-of-the-century boyhood days, he recalled catching tadpoles in Dr. Battle's lily pond down in the park, as well as "Taking a Walk in Battle's Park" being "one of the things you did, especially on Sunday."

One spring a student of mine told me she had glanced out her dormitory room that morning and just then had seen a hawk gliding by with a squirrel in its talons, and that this had made her remember that nature was all around her and always at work, whether she was paying attention or not. We dwell so much in the built environment that it is easy for even the most thoughtful to forget what a remarkable chain of being links us all. Even the university's sylvan central campus—McCorkle Place and Polk Place—with its lines of spreading oaks is a made and manicured place. That hawk was heading for the relative wilderness of Battle Park with dinner at hand, about to be, in Tennyson's words, a part of "Nature red in tooth and claw."

I had always thought Battle Park was safe forever, till back in the Eighties a plan emerged from inside the university itself to shoot a road through it, tear up a few neighborhoods too, all in the name of increasing the efficiency of the flow of vehicular traffic. That plan astonished so many so quickly that the document and its authors all but disappeared—for the moment.

In an earlier time, not too long after Dr. Battle's death, there was a volunteer squadron of protectors, defenders, and path repairers who called themselves the Battle Park Rangers. I do not know when the Rangers mustered for the last time, but I know that a plan—supported by Professor Horace Williams—to cut Battle Park and thereby reap timber profits fell by the way in that same era.

One of Horace Williams's best students, Thomas Wolfe, was also for a spell a renter of Dr. Battle's. Wolfe stayed in a small cottage on the grounds of Senlac, now the Baptist Student Union, very close to the sandy boulder that marks the westernmost point of the park, and it was Wolfe who later wrote of Chapel Hill that "the wilderness crept up to it like a beast."

Most of what is left of that beast in Chapel Hill is in Battle Park, and one of the great pleasures of walking in this town is still just stepping off a gravel road shoulder and entering our biggest woods. One spring evening, my son Hunter and I were abroad in the park, and on our way back out to Forest Theatre he ran ahead of me, into a quarter acre of periwinkle that the late-day sun was reflecting off. At my transfixion he stood there laughing like some wild sprite in a field of silver, till a cloud came across the sun and sent that vision forever into the phantom world. And one hot summer day, as Hunter ran up the mountain to Piney Prospect for the third time, just to test his nerve and his blood against the high hill, against his own best time, I waited with a watch in hand at the southwestern edge of Battle Park, wondering as all parents do about the future and their children's future.

And well I might. The older of the two boys I met at the stone seat atop the hill, Bobby Scott, who taught me to play the piano just a year after that first meeting, was now dead, having collapsed years ago while out for a run in his neighborhood not ten miles from where I stood. Yet I see him—and myself at Hunter's age—whenever I visit Dr. Battle's stone seat, and I am flooded with gratitude that he and his brother were there, glad for their meeting and for their enthusiastic telling of the old Dromgoole legend and their including me in the spirit of this place. Looking beyond my own time, I am glad too that the commanders of Wheeler's army called it a day in the spring of '65 and shed no more Southern blood here in these woods, for already they bore with them wounded and dying from a skirmish in the New Hope swamps below this mountain, one of whom was buried in Cornelia Spencer's garden up in town just a few days before Johnston's surrender to Sherman at Bennett Place.

And I am grateful for this now in Battle Park . . . for a few moments in July, when Hunter was a boy alone in the big woods and nothing—as they say—*got* him, nothing spoke to him except the exuberance and vitality of the deep green summer woods, and when the last time running he bested himself in the contest he had invented, he did so pounding apace past his father, shouting over his shoulder a winded "How'd I do?"

I told him and he was thrilled, and when I gestured at Battle's woods as we were walking out of it through a pine stand, saying "Ain't it great?" he nodded yes, still too winded to talk. So it was, and so may it always be, for as Dr. Battle well knew, the paths he blazed in this forest lead not only to its other side, but also to a wilderness of the heart where all of us must linger from time to time.

BLAND SIMPSON is the author of seven books, including *Into the Sound Country* (with photography by Ann Cary Simpson) and *The Coasts of Carolina* (with photography by Scott Taylor). A member of the Tony Award-winning string band, the Red Clay Ramblers, he is professor of English and Creative Writing at the University of North Carolina at Chapel Hill.

The Sisters' Garden

D.G. MARTIN

THERE IS A SMALL SIGN in the yard of a modest home on one of Chapel Hill's loveliest streets. It says simply, *The Garden Is Open.*

Beginning in the early spring, people from all over town find an excuse to drive down Gimghoul Road. Hundreds of walkers and joggers from the nearby campus pass by. When the sign is out, many will make at least a short stop to savor the color or the scents of the changing displays of flowers and plants that fill the garden.

Although the garden has long been a favorite springtime attraction for people who live in Chapel Hill, word is spreading. Folks come from near and far. It is a regular stop for television reporters looking for colorful springtime stories. A hotel in the town's Meadowmont neighborhood displays a glorious picture of the garden on Gimghoul Road in each of its 147 bedrooms. Only a photo of the Old Well and a composite poster of distinctive doors and entryways in the town share this honored placement.

How does a private garden become such a popular public attraction?

I decide to ask the owners to explain it to me. I walk the short distance from my house to 723 Gimghoul Road, a street that shares its name with a secret society of university students and alumni. The Gimghouls meet in a castle located at the end of the road. A couple of blocks before the castle, I reach the garden and home of Bernice Wade and Barbara Stiles. They are sitting on the front porch, smiling broadly and vibrantly, welcoming me. They seem ageless, and they look almost exactly alike.

They are sisters, of course, and twins, too. So while the garden has no official name, the neighbors call it "the sisters' garden" or "the twins' garden."

The sisters were born April 20, 1915, and they celebrate it every spring. "Actually," says Bernice, "we will have our party a little early because the height of the garden, in our minds, comes during the second week in April when the dogwoods bloom and the azaleas are at their peak."

"And don't forget the tulips," Barbara chimes in. "Tulips are our extravagance. We treat them as annuals and replace them every year."

The twin sisters talk of plans for the displays of daffodils, forget-me-nots, irises, and columbine, as if they were fireworks operators getting ready for the Fourth of July. Indeed, in April, their garden does explode in dramatic colors that no fireworks show could duplicate.

Although early April may be the garden's most stunning time, there is something in almost every season to bring visitors back. In the warm summer time, for instance, Bernice tells me, "We try new things." The twin sisters experiment with different annuals to try to find the right combination of colors, ones that their visitors will find pleasant.

A neighbor walking his dog looks up to the porch and greets the sisters, "How are things going?" The sisters wave and smile in reply.

Barbara tells me, "We love to sit here on the porch or work in the garden and watch our neighbors walk by. Or the joggers or walkers who go down the street. They always look at the garden and wave when they see us. The garden keeps us in touch."

A few years ago, one of the sisters' neighbors, Pam Pease, wrote and illustrated a book about them and their garden. Her beautiful children's book, entitled *The Garden Is Open*, tells how a garden can bring joy to an entire town. In the center of the book is a pop-up model of the sisters' house surrounded by the garden.

The book's title reminds me about that sign. "Where did 'The Garden Is Open' sign come from?" I ask. The sisters explain how they want to let everyone know that visitors do not need special permission to come into the garden, walk around, and enjoy its colors and fragrances.

Then Barbara laughs, clears her throat, and tells me softly, as if it is a secret, "We got the sign about fifteen years ago. People were so nice. They would knock on the door or call to ask permission to walk through the garden—just when we were taking a nap. We just wanted to say, 'Don't call, don't knock, just come.'"

"The sign lets them know they don't have to knock, and when we're napping, we hope they won't," says Bernice.

I ask the sisters how their garden came to be.

"The idea might have started back in the dry country of Arizona where we grew up," Bernice explains. "We had a honeysuckle vine growing up our chimney. We thought it was a treasure. When spring came and the blooms came out, our neighbors would always have a party to celebrate and come look at its beauty. When I first came to Chapel Hill and saw so many honeysuckle vines growing in our backyard, I thought I was so lucky."

Later, even after spending months and months clearing the honeysuckle out of her Chapel Hill yard, she still remembered the joy that the plant's blooms and fragrance brought to her as a girl.

Bernice moved into the house at 723 Gimghoul Road in 1944. Her husband, North Carolina native Rogers Wade, had been in the service. After his discharge he got a job as office manager at Blue Cross and Blue Shield in Chapel Hill. Rogers and Bernice would raise their two daughters in this house, and Rogers would one day become acting president of the company.

Right away, Bernice began to garden. On the porch with Barbara and me, Bernice reminisces:

> In the winter of 1944, this front yard was full of old cornstalks and clay mounds, the remnants of the former owner's victory garden. The backyard was a tangle of my honeysuckle vines and trees. Alongside the house was a gully-washed driveway and a giant oak tree.
>
> That spring, Richard Fikes brought his mule over to plow the front yard under. Then he planted black-eyed peas. Just when the neighborhood children were ready to pick the peas, he came back with his mule and plowed the peas under. He fashioned a roller from an old oil drum and rolled it down and planted grass.
>
> In the meantime, I had ordered seeds of almost every flower that Burpee's catalog offered and planted them all that spring. Some of the directions called for the seeds to be covered with fine soil, of which we had none. So I got out a kitchen sifter, and made my own.
>
> And Rogers and I brought back a carload of azaleas from Wilmington.
>
> By summer, I had my first garden. That is, the front lawn and flower garden were established. But the backyard was a jungle. It took much more time.

"See that oak tree?" Bernice points to a tree at the edge of the front yard. "It wasn't here then. Just grew up as a volunteer. But there was an ancient oak tree on the other side," she says, gazing at a raised bed full of colorful flowers. "But Hurricane Hazel brought it down, and it covered the yard of our across-the-street neighbor. Our mother gave me a magnolia tree to plant in its place."

The magnolia their mother had given Bernice grew for almost thirty years, "until it got sick and we had to take it down—about fifteen years ago. When it came down, our yard was flooded with sunlight and we decided to replace it with the flower bed. Before we planted, we brought in truck loads of soil and mulch."

The bright flowers that now grow in the place of the old oak and their mother's magnolia are gentle reminders that the twins know what they are doing and that their garden has been here a long, long time.

In 1978, Rogers Wade was very ill. Barbara, who had traveled the world as an official of the Girl Scouts, came to stay for a little while to help her sister. She never left—and lives in the "mother-in-law" apartment that adjoins the house.

"We like to keep our independence," Barbara explains. "But we like to have lunch together. And the gardening work is a joint project."

I wonder about their decision-making process. "Who has the final say-so?" I ask.

"It never comes to that," Bernice says softly. "We look things over together, talk about it, try one thing and then another, put it aside, and come back to it, and we will always come to the same conclusion. For instance, with the azaleas, we've kept moving them as they grow, as we tried to get the right flow of color, blending the pinks, the corals, and the reds. Every year we would have to ask, 'Which azaleas do we have to move this year?'"

I lean back in my chair and wonder out loud, "Why would you two work so hard all these years making a garden so pleasant and so open just for the enjoyment of whoever wants to come?"

Barbara answers, smiling almost matter-of-factly, "That's easy. As long as we have the garden, we'll never be lonely."

D.G. MARTIN is host of UNC–TV's "North Carolina Bookwatch," the state's premier literary series, and of the "Who's Talking" program on WCHL–1360. His book, *Interstate Eateries,* is based on a series of articles he wrote for *Our State Magazine.*

A Chapel Hill Walkabout

MARCIE COHEN FERRIS

WE FOUND OUR HOME in Chapel Hill on a walk. We were here for a job interview for my husband Bill in 2002. After his job talk, we went to a UNC football game where we smiled, shook hands, schmoozed, and attended a dinner the history department hosted. We had coffee on the lawn at Weaver Street Market in Carrboro, surrounded by pumpkins, bins of apples, and hula-hoopers. I thought, "We can live here." Then we met our intrepid realtor, who showed us many wonderful houses. But none felt quite like us.

When we woke Sunday morning, I took the house-hunting expedition in hand. We only had a few hours before our flight back to Washington, DC, and I said to Bill, "We're going on a walk." We began at McCorkle Place, the beautiful green on the UNC campus that softens the border between campus and downtown bars and T-shirt shops. I scoped the situation. Where do people live who walk to campus, have dogs, and want a good cup of coffee and a newspaper available by foot? I could see where. Southern Colonials, Victorians, Craftsman-style bungalows, and nineteenth- and early twentieth-century cottages were hiding behind the impressive fraternity and sorority houses on Franklin Street.

"Let's go get a house," I said, with steely resolve. We crossed Franklin Street, walked down Hillsborough Street, and hooked a right on North Street. "These are friendly houses," I said to Bill. We saw a *For Sale* sign at the top of Mint Springs Lane that looked vaguely familiar. We had come by here the day before, but were a bit too dazed to look closely at the home. "This is it," I said. "It's walking distance from campus, and the name feels good. We need to live on Mint Springs Lane."

As we left Chapel Hill, we took a quick swing through the neighborhood. Our realtor had told us, "Faculty used to live here," as though describing a far-away time before faculty became extinct or moved to more child-friendly developments. We made an offer on the house at Mint Springs Lane while standing in the security line at the Raleigh-Durham airport. Faculty were returning to the neighborhood.

We moved to Chapel Hill the following summer, and our dog Trace came with us. She was seven years old—a German shepherd mix who had lived with us in Oxford, Mississippi, and Washington. We named her after the Natchez Trace, where we found her as an abandoned puppy near the farm where Bill grew up outside Vicksburg. She became our walking companion and the dog love of my life. Daily walks with Trace deepened our connection to each place we lived, but none more so than Chapel Hill.

Before our moving boxes were unpacked, Trace and I located our daily walking route. Within a few weeks, we had found several alternatives, because the same walk gets too boring. Besides, walks serve different functions: We needed a quick, daily morning walk for Trace before I went off to teach at UNC—this was the Tenney Circle–Rosemary Street loop—and we took longer, more adventuresome walks on weekends.

Our weekend walk often took us to Battle Park—ninety-three acres of upland forest on the eastern end of the UNC campus. (Because I am snake-a-phobic, we like the park most in the fall and winter, enjoying its transition from a canopy of gold to bare trees against a Carolina blue sky.) The university has owned the forest since the late 1790s. Today the park is managed by the North Carolina Botanical Garden, whose director

Peter White describes it as a "forest of continuity," because "these woods were woods in 1800, and in 1700 and 1600." Who doesn't need a "forest of continuity" to walk through occasionally? We entered the park just behind the Forest Theatre, a magnificent stone amphitheater built into the hillside by WPA workers in the 1940s.

Trace, Bill, and I eventually had a new member of the household, Roper, an exuberant white lab, nicknamed "the love sponge," who joined us on walks to the historic Gimghoul Road–Glandon Drive neighborhood. We would stop for a quick rest at the bench at Sisters' Corner, an area dedicated by neighbors to long-time residents and twin sisters on their ninetieth birthday in 2005. Their sisterhood and the love felt by the neighbors for these master gardeners make me kind of weepy every time I read the plaque placed at the corner in their honor: "In tribute to Bernice Wade and Barbara Stiles who have made our neighborhood radiant with flowers. From their Gimghoul neighbors and friends."

When Trace was younger, she loved as long a walk as I was willing to take. She had graceful long legs and was incredibly well behaved on a leash. She was lovely around other dogs, and I took pride in her respectful greetings to both pets and their human parents. Once we entered Battle Park, I let her off-leash, and she ran ahead and waded in the creek. Trace loved water, especially on a hot day. She loved to lie under and on top of every water sprinkler we encountered. She stretched out like a sphinx and squashed numerous sprinklers until she cooled down.

Over time, she began to limp after our long walks. I realized she was aging, a fact I could never quite accept. She still looked and acted like a pup. At Christmas in 2008, Trace was diagnosed with lymphoma, and thus began a year of treatment. We had many good days, and many difficult days, until she let us know she was too tired to continue. Trace left Bill, Roper, and me on December 1, 2009. I have never experienced such wrenching pain. She loved completely, without judgment. After she was gone, I became aware of the constant conversation we shared each day and evening, without ever saying anything.

Trace always responded to storms. She would hide under Bill's desk or under our bed. We believed rough weather reminded her of her puppy-hood on the Natchez Trace. Even today when winds swirl about our house, I look for Trace. I often feel her presence. Her spirit has come inside to be with us for a few moments. Her ashes are buried in a grove just below our house, where we planted rosemary given by our friend Meredith, and hung wind chimes from my parents on the branches of a tree.

Through Trace and eventually Roper, we met our neighborhood dogs and their parents, such as Kody, the spirited black lab, and his dad who live just through the woods. Almost daily on our walks in the neighborhood, Roper and I see Moses, the Shih Tzu. When I need a visit with his mom, Sandi, I try to imagine her into existence, and she appears, coming around the corner of Tenney Circle. If it is cold out, Moses is dressed in a plaid wool coat. Roper, now an exuberant three-year-old, jumps on Sandi's beautiful white wool coat with muddy paws, and knocks Sandi's coffee mug out of her hand. It's become a ritual. The horror, the apologies, the barking. Sandi is always dressed with great style at eight in the morning. A talented painter, she spends several weeks in Florence each year, and returns with an Italian sensibility expressed in her beautiful pashmina scarves and antique gold earrings.

On the day of Trace's death, I took Roper for an early morning walk before our compassionate veterinarian was to arrive at our home. Again, I tried to will Sandi into existence. She appeared. As she approached, she called, "Good morning! How are you?" I crumbled. "This is *not* a good day, Sandi." I started to cry. "We have to put Trace down today. I can't stand it." She let me cry on her shoulder for several minutes — again, messing up her beautiful coat and scarf. Another neighbor drove by and slowed to say hello. I've always wondered if he thought something like, "Women. Dogs. Crying. Move away quickly."

Trace and Roper introduced us to the cockapoo, Teddy, and his parents Beth and Francois. When Roper sees Beth on our walk, she gets so excited she does huge helicopter-twirly jumps in the air. Roper continues these acrobatics while Beth and I chat, and even after I say goodbye and move down the street. Then Roper enjoys a wild moment or two with Scout, the lab, and his mom Julia. Biscuit, another happy white lab, also lives on Tenney Circle. Roper and Biscuit are family, raised by the same breeder on the Albemarle Sound. They greet and turn into a wagging pile of white lab.

We meet Maggie, a beautiful lumbering yellow lab, and her grandparents, Kitty and Don, who Maggie stays with while her parents are away. Roper loves Maggie with the kind of love that only a young lab can have for an older, wiser lab. Seeing Maggie is the best moment of the best day for Roper. Maggie finds Roper mildly interesting for about thirty seconds. As Roper's leash becomes impossibly tangled in my legs, I toss doggie treats wildly in the air and try to appear as if I am a normal person on a walk.

We then come upon James and Susan as they begin their jog through the neighborhood. They're so friendly. I try to warn them that Roper is really exuberant. But it is too late. Roper licks the former UNC chancellor fully in the face and knocks him off balance. "Good dog, Roper," he says. "Whoa there!" Again, the horror, the apologies, the barking.

As we come down Boundary Street and turn right on North, we stop and say hello to Holly, an adorable bronze-colored labradoodle owned by Tom and Jean. Holly polices the corner and greets all people and dogs who come within a few yards of this busy intersection. When Holly was a puppy, we watched as she dragged the contents of her family's front porch onto the lawn for chewing.

Both Trace and Roper love the neighborhood park the Giduz family created next to their home on Tenney Circle in the 1960s. If we walk by early in the morning, the lively family of deer that enjoy the protection of the neighborhood woods—not to mention the tender flowers and shrubs in our gardens—quietly graze. They blend into the winter landscape so completely that Roper hears them shuffling before she sees them. A quirky, handmade sign posted at the top of the park on a tree-turned-totem-pole reads, *Burnham Park—Enjoy It, Respect It.* The deer would like to add one more line, *Nibble It.*

A more temporary landmark was the first Obama sign that appeared in our neighborhood in 2008. It was early in the campaign, and Obama signs and bumper stickers were non-existent in Chapel Hill. That was no problem for our neighbor Margaret, who proudly made her own hand-colored *Obama for President* signs and hung them on telephone poles and in her windows. They were classics. She gave us a steady supply of Obama buttons that read *Old White Woman for Obama.*

Art has also played an important part on our walks. Bill, Roper, and I created an impromptu art installation one day. As we walked by the impressive grounds of the Venable Coker home and gardens on North Street, Roper stopped to sniff the tiger lilies. Lying among the flowers was a single, orange, spiky, suede heel. I looked a bit more and found the mate to the shoe. Nearby lay an almost empty beer bottle. One abandoned shoe—not much story. A pair of abandoned shoes—a story. A pair of abandoned, orange suede shoes with a beer bottle? Definitely a story.

We agreed these objects needed to be reunited. We positioned the shoes and beer bottle just so on the stone wall and soon forgot about them. Then rumors began to fly. We saw other walkers gather in front of the installation, talking, scratching their heads. The shoe art became a neighborhood collaboration. Yellow roses appeared in the beer bottle and were replaced with fresh flowers when they faded. Months later, someone added weather-resistant plastic roses to the assemblage. The latest addition is a small stuffed animal, propped comfortably between the now-faded shoes. It has been several years since *Shoes* appeared, and I often stop and adjust the objects after a particularly windy night. Each time I approach it, I wonder if an upright citizen will have removed it or at least brought it up for heated discussion in a Chapel Hill Town Council meeting. ("Enough already with the orange suede heels, the beer bottle, the flowers, the stuffed animals! Where will it end?!") No worries, though. When they do take it away, we will create *Shoes* 2 somewhere in the neighborhood. It is good to keep people talking.

Roper, Bill, and I enjoy walking through the Coker Arboretum, a five-acre outdoor classroom created in 1903 by Dr. William Chambers Coker, UNC's first botany professor. It is a beautiful setting for quiet contemplation, study, weddings, and family photographs, a place where Roper has terrified innumerable children and disturbed several nuptials. She likes to splash in the arboretum's water features. In the fall, we eat persimmons that have fallen from the tree at the corner of Battle and Hooper Lane. As the season progresses, Bill throws a branch high up into the tree, and the last remaining persimmons tumble to the ground. Roper eats them like candy.

On occasion, we venture out of our neighborhood and walk downtown. But it is not so easy with Roper's exuberance. She considers every person we pass as family, and if we encounter a strange dog, she has an out-of-body experience that demands great strength and a calmer demeanor than my own to control. When we slowly pass Ye Olde Waffle Shoppe on Franklin Street, I smell the pancakes and hash browns. I stop and look at the posters of UNC's sports teams in the window of Sutton's Drug Store and wish I could go in and eat a cheeseburger and fries like they do. In the first months of the Iraq War in 2003, the chalkboard that hung in the front window of Pepper's Pizza advertised their politically astute bargain, "Tomahawk Missile, $1,000,000. Slice of pepperoni, $2.30."

Walking helps me keep things in perspective. I go outside with Roper, her leash tightly wound around my wrist in a very un-Cesar Millan fashion, and try to clear my head of life's daily anxieties. "Focus on the trees and the blue sky," I tell myself. "Breathe." Roper leaps for a squirrel, and then sees an unfamiliar dog in the distance. We lunge forward.

MARCIE COHEN FERRIS is an associate professor of American Studies at the University of North Carolina at Chapel Hill. Her book, *Matzoh Ball Gumbo: Culinary Tales of the Jewish South*, was nominated for a 2006 James Beard Foundation Award.

Views from Before 🎇

The Presidents Come to Chapel Hill

WILLIAM E. LEUCHTENBURG

I.

IN THE LATE SPRING OF 1847, a current of excitement ran through Chapel Hill: The president of the United States was coming to town. No such event had ever happened before. Moreover, he was a very special president. Though now of Tennessee, James K. Polk was a Tar Heel born (Mecklenburg County) and a Tar Heel bred, Carolina Class of 1818.

As a student, Polk had made an impression less by native intelligence than by the way he applied himself. To clinch an argument, his fellow students would say the point they were making was as surely true as "that Jim Polk will get up in the morning at first call." An indefatigable self-starter, he was graduated with highest honors in both mathematics and classics; delivered a commencement oration in Latin; and finished first in his class. Since there were only fourteen students in the class, that may not seem much of a distinction. But consider that one of his classmates would become the first governor of Florida; another, paymaster-general of the United States and consul general in Italy; another, president of Davidson

College; yet another, bishop of Mississippi and chancellor of the University of the South. Among his fellow students in his Chapel Hill years were two future governors of North Carolina (one of them John Motley Morehead), as well as the future presiding officers of the Virginia and North Carolina Senates and the secretary of the navy who would be with Polk on his historic visit to Chapel Hill in 1847.

At eight in the morning on a warm spring day, the president and his entourage left Raleigh in a dozen carriages and other conveyances bound for Chapel Hill, a trip that required nine hours. He stopped often at farms to rest the horses and to shake hands with well-wishers, and took midday dinner along the route. Not until nearly evening did he arrive at the Eagle Hotel in Chapel Hill where, in his honor, the proprietor, Nancy Hilliard, had constructed an annex to house him and his companions. His large party included a naval officer: the brilliant Matthew Fontaine Maury—who was to win renown as "Pathfinder of the Seas"—the father of modern oceanography.

After checking in at Miss Nancy's, Polk strolled to campus, where at the chapel, Gerrard Hall, he responded graciously—though with characteristic ponderousness—to an address of welcome from the president of the university, David Lowry Swain. It was "to the acquisitions received" at this university, Polk said, "I mainly attribute whatever success has attended the labor of my subsequent life." Afterwards, he spoke to the only professor from his student years who remained: the noted scientist Elisha Mitchell, after whom Mt. Mitchell is named. Over the next two days, Polk renewed acquaintance with the campus. Accompanied by college chums, he reconnoitered the buildings of his youth, and with his wife returned to his old dorm room on the top floor of South Building, which had been completed only the year before he arrived as a student.

Polk's stay came to a climax on Commencement Day, a magnet for hundreds of visitors. The correspondent for the *New York Herald* reported: "The little village of Chapel Hill is overflowing with people and they continue to pour in from all quarters, a number of persons having arrived all the way from Tennessee. There are tents pitched and wagons occupied by visitors, as at a camp meeting, for want of accommodations in the houses, which are filled to their fullest capacity, 'Miss Nancy' having the prospect of a thousand guests for dinner." After observing the Class of 1847 graduated, the president returned to the White House, where he entered in his diary: "& thus ended my excursion to the University of N. Carolina. It was an exceedingly agreeable one."

II.

While Polk was on campus, his secretary of state, James Buchanan, wrote him every day to report on affairs in Washington, so it was altogether fitting that twelve years later Buchanan would be the next president to go to Chapel Hill. The chance to get away came at a propitious time. In the 1858 elections, his party had suffered brutal losses. Afterwards, he wrote, "Well! we have met the enemy . . . & we are theirs. . . . Our crushing defeat . . . is so great that it is almost absurd." At the same time that his party was disintegrating, his personal life was falling to pieces. Kate Thompson, the wife of his secretary of the interior, Jacob Thompson, called Buchanan a "hardened old Bachelor," which he was, but he also craved female companionship. Unhappily for him, his younger sister Harriet, who had been serving as a surrogate First Lady, abandoned him for three months, and another resident of the White House — a widow for whom Buchanan expressed some fondness — also left town. Increasingly irritable, the lonely president, his biographer writes, "got on the nerves of his associates," and as a result some cabinet members "tried to get him out of Washington and cooked up a presidential tour to the South." Consequently, on May 30, 1859, Buchanan departed for Baltimore where he sailed to Norfolk and then moved on to Chapel Hill.

He did so at a perilous moment in the history of the republic, with Southern voices calling for dismemberment of the union growing every day more strident. The university itself was being shaken by the controversy over slavery. Three years earlier, the precocious young head of the chemistry department had revealed innocently that he favored the Free Soil candidate for president. That comment triggered his dismissal. Students burned him in effigy and planned to tar and feather him. A North Carolina newspaper declared that no man who supported a candidate opposed to the expansion of slavery "ought to be allowed to breathe the air or tread the soil of North Carolina." To escape a mob of three hundred in Salisbury, he was compelled to flee secretly during the night on a northbound train, leaving behind forever his native state and the home he had built in Chapel Hill—a place we know today as the Horace Williams House.

144

Though Buchanan, who truckled to slaveholders, bore no small part of the responsibility for bringing on the secession crisis, he identified himself, at a stop on his southbound train, as one who was "a supporter of the Constitution and the Union and . . . ever expect to be." He thanked God there was no danger to the Constitution from North Carolina, a sentiment that produced "loud and prolonged cheers"—to which he responded, "God bless the Old North State."

Buchanan and his party, including Secretary Thompson, one of two UNC graduates Buchanan had named to his cabinet, made the trip from Raleigh to Chapel Hill on an oppressively hot day—at first on a train drawn by four locomotives, then by stage. Upon arrival, Buchanan was led to President Swain's yard. "The reception and open-air dinner on the beautiful lawn of the president's mansion were notable," the mathematics professor and man of letters, Archibald Henderson, later wrote. "The tables beneath the shade of the mighty oaks were . . . loaded with fruits, confectioneries, and Southern delicacies of every description." At the commencement exercises, Buchanan heard a series of orations by students. One, a young man from New York, spoke on the subject, "The Persecution of the Jews," and, it was recorded, "dwelt at length upon the unblushing and repeated acts of enmity exhibited towards an unoffending people." Nearly two dozen newspapermen descended on Chapel Hill for the occasion—from the Carolinas, from Richmond, from Washington, and from as far away as New York City. They had a miserable time of it, traveling from the depot in Durham on a wagon without springs that moved at a tortoise pace — a grueling trip of six hours. But once they reached the campus, they were impressed. The commencement exercises, noted one correspondent, were "staged upon a sylvan theater surrounded by dense forests . . . one of the best selected sites for an institution of learning that can be found in the whole country."

The venture did Buchanan a world of good. The press found him "gay and frisky as a young buck," and a cabinet official reported that "the old gentleman was perfectly delighted with his trip. . . . There has not been since the days of Genl. Jackson such an ovation to any President." At the close of the commencement ceremonies, President Swain announced that Buchanan would receive callers under the Davie Poplar. Beneath the tree, the silver-haired president of the United States not only "had quite a pleasant time" shaking hands with "the many fair ladies who were introduced to him" but kissed one "very pretty young lady" and deputized her to kiss all of the rest of the women on his behalf. Afterwards, Kate Thompson, who got an accounting of the journey from her husband, wrote, "Truly, I think the old Rip Van Winkle waked up for this occasion. . . . He had a good time in N. Carolina for Mr. T. says he kissed hundreds of pretty girls which made his mouth water!"

Yet amidst the frivolity, Buchanan uttered a prophetic warning. If he could speak to all young men in the land, he told his Chapel Hill audience, he would "advise them to devote themselves to the preservation of the principles of the Constitution, for without those blessings, our liberties are gone." He added:

> Let this Constitution be torn to atoms; let thirty republics rise up against each other; let the Union separate, and it would be the most fatal day for the liberties of the human race that ever dawned upon any land. Let this experiment be tried, and mankind and every friend would deplore the sad event. I belong to a passing generation.

My lamp of life cannot continue long. I hope I may survive to the end of my Presidential term, but so emphatically do I believe that mankind . . . are interested in the preservation of the Union that I hope I may be gathered to my fathers before I should witness its dissolution.

Buchanan spoke these words less than two years before the firing on Fort Sumter, an event with awful consequences for the university. Cornelia Phillips Spencer remarked on the "sad spring of 1861" that "besides innumerable violets and jessamines brought into bloom," there emerged "a strange enormous and terrible flower, the blood-red flower of war." Scores of Carolina students who had greeted Polk, who had cheered Buchanan, would lose their lives on the battlefield. "The sad tale of the fallen," one writer later noted, "begins with Lt. William Preston Mangum at Bull Run and ends with Capt. John H.D. Fain and J. J. Phillips on the retreat from Petersburg. It includes five at Shiloh, fourteen at Malvern Hill, nine at Sharpsburg, eight at Fredericksburg, five at Chancellorsville, four at Vicksburg, seven at Chickamauga, six at the Wilderness, five at Spottsylvania Court House, nine in the Atlanta campaign, twenty-one at Gettysburg."

III.

When, in 1867, President Andrew Johnson came to Chapel Hill, the perdurable president of the university, David Swain, welcomed him. It was not their first encounter, for in May 1865 Swain had been one of North Carolina's three delegates who had met with Johnson to discuss the Reconstruction regime. The two men shared a common lot, for both were loathed by Confederate sympathizers. Johnson was viewed as a renegade. A Southerner, he had supported the Union in the Civil War. Swain, son of a Massachusetts man, was vilified as a traitor. He had secured from General William Tecumseh Sherman, formerly superintendent of the State Military Academy of Louisiana, a pledge, "as one college president to another," that the University of North Carolina would not be harmed, and that promise had been kept. But, on learning of Swain's negotiations with Sherman, Jefferson Davis had ordered the president of the university arrested, if he could be apprehended, and a Confederate general in the closing days of the war, as his infantry division marched down Franklin Street, had cried that Swain should be hanged.

By the time President Johnson arrived on campus in 1867, he had ingratiated himself with some adherents to the Lost Cause by his stout, though unsuccessful, resistance to Northern demands for military occupation of the South, but Swain was unforgiven. It had been he who, after arranging for the surrender of Raleigh, had turned over the keys to the capitol to Sherman's agent. Still worse, his daughter Ellie, following a scandalously brief courtship, had outraged the Chapel Hill community by marrying one of Sherman's commanders. To disrupt the wedding ceremony, students had tolled bells for three hours and had hanged David Swain in effigy from the bell tower of Old South.

In response to an address of greeting from Swain, Johnson recalled that this was not his first visit to the village. He remembered that forty-one years earlier, as an impoverished seventeen-year-old tailor's apprentice, he had run away from his master in his hometown of Raleigh in quest of a new life in Tennessee. On his way west, he had walked the main thoroughfare to Chapel Hill, where he wandered down Franklin Street footsore and famished. When he came to the outskirts of the village, he had "begged for supper and lodging." The young stranger was not only taken in and treated kindly, but, on leaving, given bread and meat to sustain him on his long trek toward the mountains. In the years since, Johnson had, with the help of his wife, learned to read, had pursued his trade of tailor, had risen in the ranks of the Democratic Party, had been chosen by Lincoln to be military governor of Tennessee, had been elected vice president of the United States, and, as a consequence of John Wilkes Booth's bullet, had succeeded Lincoln in the White House. This time, on his second visit to Chapel Hill, he came from Raleigh not on foot but by special train to Durham and then by carriage, not as a penniless lad but as the holder of the highest office in the land. In Chapel Hill, he found that the cabin that had sheltered him was still standing. Speaking from the front steps of the Swain mansion, President Johnson concluded: "North Carolina has not been, in the language of school men, exactly my alma mater, but still she is my mother and, God bless her, I am proud of her."

With Johnson in Chapel Hill were three well-known public figures: Secretary of State William Seward, Postmaster-General Alexander Randall, and General Dan Sickles. The Philanthropic Society resolved to make members of Seward and Randall, though this gesture of good will occasioned unexpected difficulty. When the president of the society put the traditional question: "Do you promise to keep the by-laws and transactions of this society a secret?" all save one of the dozen inductees gave their assent and took their seats. Seward remained standing. After an awkward moment, he said: "I do not. I never joined a secret society in my life. I was an anti-Mason and an anti-Know Nothing. I am an anti-secret society man."

A generation later, one who was in the room that day recalled what ensued:

> Absolute consternation followed this announcement. Nobody knew what to do or say, or what would happen next. Just when it seemed as if the entire society would collapse Fabius Haywood Busbee, a very bright and fertile boy who is now the attorney of the Southern Railway at Raleigh . . . arose and said: "Mr. President, I move the Constitution and by-laws be suspended in the case of Mr. Seward." The president put the motion, which he had no right to do, as the constitution . . . provided that it should never be suspended . . . except upon six weeks' notice, and it was carried by Busbee's vote, everybody else being too dumfounded to cast their ballots. That's the way William H. Seward became a member of the Philanthropic Society.

Dan Sickles proved to be the subject of far greater controversy. The Dialectic Society had no problem with inducting President Johnson, but it drew the line at Sickles. The Di's might well have found him unworthy because of his egregious behavior. When he learned in 1859 that his young wife was carrying on an affair with a Washington dandy, he forced her to write out a confession saying that in a house on Washington's Fifteenth Street, "I did what is usual for a wicked woman to do" and had "an intimacy of an improper kind . . . in the parlor, on the sofa." Sickles then hunted down the rake, Philip Barton Key, son of the author of "The Star Spangled Banner." At Lafayette Square near the White House, crying "Key, you scoundrel, you have dishonored my bed—you must die!" he gunned Key down in cold blood as his victim pleaded for mercy. Sickles then took his wife back into his marriage bed, an act that outraged polite society far more than his original deed. If he could be so forgiving, then why had he murdered in the first place? The Whig diarist George Templeton Strong was later to say of Sickles: "One might as well try to spoil a rotten egg as to damage Dan's character." The dissident Di's, then, had good reason for blackballing Sickles. They may well have done so, though, not because they disapproved of his frayed character but rather to protest his role as military governor of the Carolinas. Sickles, scoundrel though he was, championed the rights of the freedman.

In the wake of this contretemps, the 1867 commencement came almost as an anticlimax. Only nine years earlier, the University of North Carolina boasted the largest enrollment of any university in the United States, save Yale. But when President Johnson and his party attended the 1867 commencement, the number of "distinguished guests" seated on the stage of Gerrard Hall outnumbered the graduating class—a total of only eleven in that grim postbellum year.

Andrew Johnson's visit may have had one unhappy consequence for the university. The Reconstruction governor of North Carolina, perhaps out of anger that he had not been invited to join Johnson at the commencement, removed David Swain as president. Not many days later, a horse General

Sherman had given Swain as a present bolted, hurling him to the ground. Swain did not long survive the fall.

IV.

Seventy-one years would go by before another president came to Chapel Hill while in office, but during that long interval the university received visits from one president-to-be and one president-who-had-been. In January 1909, four years before he entered the White House, Woodrow Wilson, at that time president of Princeton, spoke in Chapel Hill at the urging of his nephew, a Carolina undergraduate. At the conclusion of his address, Wilson said:

> I wish there were some great orator who could go about and make men drunk with this spirit of self-sacrifice. I wish there were some man whose golden tongue might every day carry abroad the golden accents of that creative age in which we were born a nation; accents which would ring like tones of reassurance around the whole circle of the globe, so that America might again have the distinction of showing men the way, the certain way, of achievement and confident hope.

One Carolina student in Gerrard Hall that day, a young man so short that he perched in the crowded gallery on another student's knee, was mesmerized. Those words, he thought, were aimed directly at him: the president of the senior class, Frank Porter Graham.

In 1915, William Howard Taft, only two years after leaving the White House, inaugurated the distinguished Weil Lectures on American Citizenship. Taft, who in 1912 had been the only major party candidate ever to finish third in a presidential race, welcomed a venue that would abet his desire to rehabilitate his reputation after a campaign in which Theodore Roosevelt had called him a "flubdub" and a "fathead" with less brains

150

than a guinea pig. In Bill Powell's pictorial history of the university there is a photograph of the portly ex-president, standing next to the slender Edward Kidder Graham on the front porch of the university president's house. No one looking at that picture will have difficulty in comprehending a contemporary jest—that William Howard Taft (all 332 pounds of him) once got up in a streetcar and gave his seat to three ladies.

V.

Not until a soggy day in December 1938, though, did Chapel Hill again welcome a presidential incumbent: Franklin Delano Roosevelt, who travelled north by train from the Little White House in Warm Springs, Georgia. So great was the excitement about the approaching visit that at the depot in Sanford, as the locomotive of the Seaboard's streamliner rounded the bend, ten thousand people stood in the rain to greet him. Roosevelt was scheduled to speak at Kenan Stadium, but the uncooperative weather drove the ceremonies indoors to the newly constructed Woollen Gymnasium where an overflow crowd sweltered under hot klieg lights.

The spectators in the stifling gym knew they were present at an unusual event. Roosevelt faced a battery of fifteen microphones and eight newsreel cameras, and his address was carried over 225 radio stations. Twenty telegraph wires transmitted the stories of nearly one hundred reporters, and his words—translated into French, German, Italian, and Russian—went overseas by short wave. Roosevelt came at a critical time. At home, he had just suffered so severe a defeat in the midterm elections that many doubted that the liberal outlook would long survive. Abroad, Hitler had in September humiliated the democracies at Munich. Still worse, the Nazis, on Kristallnacht, had carried out their horrifying pogrom against Jews only days before FDR's visit. Not since the midterm elections had the president delivered an address, and it was singular that he would choose Chapel Hill as his venue and to speak not at a ceremony such as a commencement but to a student forum — though one of the country's best known, the Carolina Political Union. It was clearly young people — the people who carried hope for the future — he was seeking to reach.

Roosevelt cut a wide swath on that December day. He identified himself with the university's illustrious president, Frank Porter Graham, who, like himself, had often been abused by the press; he denied reports that his favorite breakfast dish was "grilled millionaire"; he quoted Supreme Court Justice Benjamin Cardozo ("We live in a world of change. . . . there is change whether we will it or not"); and he declared that it was the University of North Carolina's recognition of that reality — "thinking and acting in terms of today and tomorrow and not in the tradition of yesterday" — that brought him so willingly to Chapel Hill. The president, who had been awarded an honorary degree, carried his address to a climax by saying:

> Because we live in an era of acceleration, we can no longer trust to the evolution of future decades to meet . . . new problems. They rise before us today, and they must be met today. . . .
>
> That is why I . . . associate myself so greatly with the younger generation. That is why I am happy and proud to become an alumnus of the University of North Carolina, typifying as it does American liberal thought through American action.

VI.

Nearly a quarter of a century elapsed before another president came to Chapel Hill, but during that period FDR cast a long shadow. At one point, he said that Dr. New Deal was giving way to Dr. Win-the-War, and it was as commander-in-chief that he most affected his successors. Six of the next seven presidents served in uniform during World War II. Two who wound up in the White House had spent time earlier in Chapel Hill.

In 1945, a navy plane carrying an admiral and his young aide crashed into a ditch at Horace Williams Airport, and from the wreckage emerged Gerald Ford. "We all got out," Ford recalled years later. "Five minutes later, it exploded and burned. We were all very fortunate." This flight marked Ford's third encounter with Chapel Hill. His first stay had come in the summer of 1938 when he had attended law classes at the university and lived in Carr Building, then a law school dorm. Four years later, the U.S. Navy had sent Ensign Ford to its Pre-Flight program on the Carolina campus—an enterprise that drilled nearly 20,000 men, including Free French forces. He was given the task of physical training instructor, an assignment for which he could hardly have been more qualified; formerly an all-star center on the University of Michigan's football team, Jerry Ford had been offered contracts by both the Green Bay Packers and the Detroit Lions. While in Chapel Hill, he may have crossed paths with another future Republican president, though neither knew that at the time.

153

When the Japanese rained death on Pearl Harbor, George Herbert Walker Bush, a student at a prestigious prep school who had been accepted at Yale, decided—against the advice of his family—to forego college for the present and volunteer for the U.S. Navy's air wing. On his eighteenth birthday in June 1942, he enlisted as a seaman second class—the first Andover boy to sign up. At New York's Pennsylvania Station, he said goodbye to his father, the patrician Wall Street investment banker, Prescott Bush, and caught a southbound train to report for duty in the Sixth Battalion, Company K, Second Platoon of the naval air program at the University of North Carolina. "I came out of a very sheltered background," he later said, "and woke up in Chapel Hill." Here he had "a rude awakening from exposure to the rest of the world." He found his platoon "a darned good-hearted bunch," he wrote home to "Mum and Dad" on their Kennebunkport estate, but was dismayed that a number of the cadets were so much "below average intelligence" that they relished being told, "Kill the Japs." The highlight of his sojourn was the day that his future bride, Barbara, a student at Ashley

Hall in Charleston, met him at the Carolina Inn, though their few hours together were marred by a drenching downpour that caused them to seek shelter in the press box of Kenan Stadium. When, after a few months of instruction, Bush, not yet nineteen, earned his wings, he became the youngest flyer in the United States Navy. Both Bush and Ford saw action in the Pacific. So, too, did two others: Lieutenant (J.G.) Richard Nixon, who no doubt made a number of trips to Chapel Hill during his three years at Duke Law School, and the next incumbent of the White House to visit the Carolina campus—PT-boat lieutenant John Fitzgerald Kennedy. (Subsequently, their commander, Dwight D. Eisenhower, the architect of D-Day, recalled numbers of visits to Chapel Hill to see his boyhood chum, Swede Haisley, who headed the Naval ROTC program on campus. In addition, when Kate Smith performed in Memorial Hall during the war, one of the members of her troupe was the rising young Hollywood star, Ronald Reagan, who had been commissioned as a uniformed public relations officer.)

The Secret Service took extraordinary measures to prepare for Kennedy's visit in October 1961 because the president had been the recipient of a number of death threats. Agents crawled through a drainage ditch and scrutinized ravines and prominent trees. Years later, Bill Friday, who greeted Kennedy that day, recorded that "they had armed guards in every square of seating throughout Kenan Stadium. Dozens and dozens under arms—you didn't know it, but they were there." And he remembered especially what the head of the Secret Service detail said to him after going over the precautions: "I just wanted to show you this because you'll be up there standing by President Kennedy, and they might miss."

Kennedy arrived in circumstances quite different from FDR's visit. While Roosevelt had come to North Carolina by train, Kennedy arrived at Raleigh-Durham Airport by jet. He rode down Highway 54 with the young governor of the state, Terry Sanford, by his side, in a limousine with a protective bubble-top that he removed when he reached the outskirts of Chapel Hill—just as, alas, he was to remove it on the streets of Dallas two years later. While Roosevelt spoke on a date of no special significance, Kennedy turned up on University Day. And while Roosevelt encountered a sullen drizzle that moved his address indoors, Kennedy met balmy Indian summer, and hence was able to talk at what the Fayetteville editor Roy Parker later called "that invigorating, indescribably poignant time of year," under a sky of "burnished crispness" in the "achingly-beautiful arena of Chapel Hill's stadium," where, in the words of another writer, "warmed by a docile sun, pensive in cap and gown," Kennedy rose to speak before forty thousand students and townspeople. Kennedy's visit was different for yet another, and more important, reason. For the first time in all the many years presidents had come to Chapel Hill, the student audience—at long last and much too late—would no longer be composed wholly of whites.

In other respects, though, their visits were similar. Like Roosevelt, Kennedy was enthusiastically welcomed. Like Roosevelt, he was awarded an honorary degree, the first he had received since taking office. (The following year in New Haven, he would receive another, responding mischievously, "Now I have the best of both worlds—a Harvard education and a Yale degree.") Like Roosevelt, too, he made a direct appeal to young people, in this instance with even more evocative imagery because the youthful president was introduced by the even younger president of the university, Bill Friday. The forty-four-year-old Kennedy—the youngest president ever elected, succeeding the then-oldest man who had ever been in the White House—had a particular attraction to the young. In the 1960 campaign in Ohio, he had said, "If we can lower the voting age to nine, we'll sweep the state."

President Kennedy, standing before a huge North Carolina flag, began his address in Kenan Stadium by saying, "North Carolina has long been identified with enlightened and progressive leaders and people." After referring to figures such as Frank Porter Graham, he remarked on the venerable tradition at Chapel Hill "that the graduate of this university is a man of his Nation as well as a man of his time." (Today he would incorporate in that statement "a woman of this nation as well as a woman of her time.") He added: "I want to emphasize, in the great concentration which we now place upon scientists and engineers, how much we still need the men and women educated in the liberal traditions, willing to take the long look, undisturbed by prejudices and slogans of the moment, who attempt to make an honest judgment on difficult events."

After these serious comments, the Harvard-educated Kennedy struck a more jocular note, drawing laughter from the crowd when he referred to himself "as a graduate of a small land grant college in Massachusetts," and then remarked, "Those of you who regard my profession of political life with some disdain should remember that it made it possible for me to move from being an obscure lieutenant in the United States Navy to Commander-in-Chief in 14 years, with very little technical competence." He also said facetiously that he would not "adopt from the Belgian constitution a provision giving three votes instead of one to college graduates — at least not until more Democrats go to college."

But he became more serious when he declared:

> I hope you will realize that from the beginning of this country, and especially in North Carolina, there has been the closest link between educated men and women and politics and government. And also to remember that our nation's first great leaders were also our first great scholars.
>
> A contemporary described Thomas Jefferson as "a gentleman of 32 who could calculate an eclipse, survey an estate, tie an artery, plan an edifice, try a cause, break a horse, dance the minuet, and play the violin." John Quincy Adams, after being summarily dismissed from the United States Senate, could then become Boylston Professor of Rhetoric and Oratory at Harvard.

Kennedy admonished:

> This is a great institution with a great tradition and with devoted alumni.
> . . . Its establishment and continued function . . . has required great sac-
> rifice by the people of North Carolina. I cannot believe that all of this is
> undertaken merely to give this school's graduates an economic advan-
> tage in the life-struggle.
>
> "A university," said Professor Woodrow Wilson, "should be an organ
> of memory for the State, for the transmission of its best traditions."
> And Prince Bismarck was even more specific. "One third of the students
> of German universities," he once said, "broke down from over-work,
> another third broke down from dissipation, and the other third ruled
> Germany."

President Kennedy then peered out at the students in the stadium
and stabbing the air with his forefinger, stated, "I leave it to each of you
to decide in which category you will fall."

VII.

Since that golden moment in 1961, only one chief executive has left the
Oval Office to speak in Chapel Hill, but he was preceded by a president-
to-be, Richard Nixon, and a former president—the 1984 Weil Lecturer,
Jimmy Carter—and followed in 2008 by a future president, Barack Obama.
Shortly before he was elected president in 1968, Nixon stopped in Chapel
Hill to consult Erwin Danziger, son of the legendary Viennese chocolatier,
Papa Danziger, and brother of the proprietor of a favorite campus hang-
out, the Rathskeller. At the UNC Computer Center, where Erwin Danziger
directed data processing, Nixon sought to learn more about a manpower
project Danziger had developed to match unemployed men and women to

jobs appropriate to their skills — a program that might serve him well in the White House. Memory is still green of the time that Senator Obama spoke at a Dean Dome rally and turned up on a basketball court for a pickup game with UNC players.

When Carter arrived with daughter Amy, a gala banquet in his honor was arranged at the Carolina Inn. After giving an address welcoming Carter, I returned to our table at the inn where a congressman's wife said to me, "It's really too bad that they've scheduled Carter for the vast space of Memorial Hall. The turnout will be pitiful. In this age of Reagan, no one is interested in Carter anymore." That seemed a sensible judgment. But when we approached Memorial Hall after the dinner, we were astonished to find that every seat had been taken, and some five hundred more people were milling on the lawn adjacent to the building. A huge throng, reported the *Daily Tar Heel*, "managed to hear by hanging from the rafters, from trees outside, and by sitting in Memorial's large window sills," with many "standing in the bushes outside Memorial Hall listening through open windows." The enthusiasm on that joyous evening was a harbinger of what lay ahead nine years later.

Well before the 200th birthday of the University of North Carolina in 1993, planners resolved that nothing would lend more éclat to the Bicentennial Observance than the participation of the president of the United States, but Bill Clinton proved to be an elusive target. "The first invitation to the new president," writes Steven Tepper in his excellent account of the occasion, "was like a stone tossed into a bottomless well." To capture the attention of the White House, everyone from Governor Jim Hunt to Dean Smith lobbied the president. "Even Pythagoras," Tepper remarks, "would have been unable to describe the number of angles we went at to secure Clinton." The clinching argument may well have been that the most recent presidential visitor had been John F. Kennedy, a hero to Clinton ever since a summer day when, as a wide-eyed sixteen-year-old representing Arkansas at the Boys Nation Convention, he had gripped Kennedy's hand in the Rose Garden.

On October 12, 1993, Air Force One touched down at RDU Airport, and a twenty-car motorcade, preceded by motorcycles flashing blue lights, took Bill Clinton to Kenan Stadium. Though the First Lady did not accompany him, she was nonetheless a presence. Outside the stadium, College Republicans carried placards reading "I Don't Trust President Clinton, or Her Husband!" and, to protest a proposed cigarette tax, a tobacco grower urged, "Stick with Hillary—Stop Screwing Farmers." On the way, the president reviewed the text of his address in which he was to say, "This university has produced enough excellence to fill a library or lead a nation," and then cite a number of Tar Heel luminaries, including Thomas Wolfe and Walker Percy. Before he could deliver these words to the thousands massed in the stadium, though, Clinton had to wait out a processional that, as Tepper has said, "was like a German opera—fully adorned and interminably long."

As I took my place in that processional, "fully adorned" in ritualistic hood and gown, I dwelt not on the tedium of delay as we shuffled along, but on what that night signified. Clinton was capping nearly two centuries of the appearance on the Carolina campus of past, present, and future presidents of the United States: Jim Polk; Jamie Buchanan; that one-time tailor's apprentice who trudged down Franklin Street, Andrew Johnson; portly Bill Taft; Woodrow Wilson who so inspired Frank Porter Graham; FDR; Ike; young Jack Kennedy; Dick Nixon; Jerry Ford; Ronald Reagan; the first George Bush; Jimmy Carter; and now Bill Clinton—the movers and shakers who led the republic and who, for nearly two centuries, walked the streets of Chapel Hill.

WILLIAM LEUCHTENBURG, William Rand Kenan Jr. professor emeritus at the University of North Carolina at Chapel Hill, is a leading scholar of the presidency. He is the author of more than a dozen books on twentieth-century American history, including *Franklin D. Roosevelt and the New Deal, 1932–1940*, winner of the Bancroft and Parkman prizes.

The War Years

THE THREE OF THEM are headed east, hitching a ride. They wear neckties, fedoras, and top coats, as travelers do in 1943, and they're grinning mischievously, there in front of Frank Graham's house.

In another time, they might be running to high school sweethearts for the weekend or craving mom's cooking; on a spring Friday they could be bound for Nags Head. But just now the world beyond Chapel Hill is upside down. Carefree college and mischief are on indefinite suspension. Three boys with a cardboard sign are going *Home To The Draft Board,* and this snapshot from the Carolina yearbook will be one of the last of them as boys.

On the campus they leave behind, the dancing will not stop. Navy cadets will toughen up on the Woollen Gym floor by day and return there by night to cut the rug, decked in their Dress Blues for the coeds and town girls and all the best big bands around. By day, a physical and academic regimen never seen at Carolina before or since; in the town, a similar sense of purpose—rationing the very basics, packing bazooka shells with gifts for Hitler and envelopes with hope and support for those boys. By night, greater vigor for "Take the 'A' Train," more passion for "Manhattan Serenade."

To the Vietnam generation, Chapel Hill was identified with a march down Franklin Street behind a banner reading, *End the War Now*. A look fifty years back left no question why the expressions of those demonstrators were anathema to so many of their parents.

Having embraced a military training entourage that dominated the campus for four years, few towns in 1940s America were as warlike as the peace-loving liberal oasis of the South. When it was over—the world all shaken out and young people's worldviews thoroughly rearranged— Chapel Hill had a lot of war stories.

After Pearl Harbor, campus friendships were made with the knowledge that your pal might vanish tomorrow, headed overseas without even the chance to say goodbye. But as young men tossed aside schoolbooks and saddle oxfords for war duty, their places were taken quickly by others in uniform.

As the storm of war shrouded Europe, UNC President Frank Porter Graham became determined that Carolina would donate its facilities to the effort. Dr. Frank told students and faculty that the university "has offered all its resources to the nation for the defense of the freedom and democracy it was founded to serve."

Because of Graham's close ties in Washington, and because the campus had an unusual wealth of athletic facilities, the U.S. Navy in 1942 chose Carolina for one of its four massive Pre-Flight Training Schools. By the war's end some 18,700 cadets had undergone rigorous dawn-to-dusk training in Chapel Hill. They took over ten dorms in the men's upper and lower quads; at times, that part of the campus was sealed off, and nighttime guards had orders to shoot anyone not answering a challenge.

The navy had the run of Caldwell and Manning halls for classrooms, Lenoir for eating, Woollen and Bowman Gray Pool, and all the surrounding fields for conditioning, Hill and Gerrard for church services.

The university could request use of its own Memorial Hall "when not in conflict with cadet activities."

Pre-Flight was only the largest military presence on campus. Carolina also hosted the navy's V-12 pre-midshipman scholastic program, a navy ROTC program, the army's geography and language study program, an army air corps meteorology program, and a unit of the marines. Of 5,300 students in the fall of 1943, 3,500 were men in uniform. The 1944 *Yack* easily could be mistaken for a military school yearbook.

Town and gown thoroughly embraced them. Businesses, still strapped by the Depression, suddenly boomed. A growing female student population found substitute friends and romances for the boys gone off to war.

"The administration and the navy did a good job of not getting in each other's way," said Bert Bennett, a confidant to several North Carolina governors who was student body president in 1942. "They needed the room, and we made it. It was a no-problem relationship."

Mostly. The navy and the university communities interacted closely, and inevitably conflicts arose. Cramped housing, crowded streets and restaurants tested a small town's patience at times. The navy's high standards produced a few fireworks. The Pre-Flight School's commander fired this blast toward university Comptroller Billy Carmichael, regarding food service in Lenoir Hall:

> The stew is too greasy . . . water's too hot, ice cream melts, beef too stringy, dishes need washing. . . . The meat was not fit for human consumption, the only redeeming feature of it was the fact that it was not tainted or spoiled.

John Foster West knows what a remarkable, world-shrinking time this was. As a student he rose at 4 AM to dish up breakfast for military trainees; as a member of the cross-country team he often jogged with a young officer. West was sitting in the audience in Memorial in November 1942 for a live

Kate Smith radio show when his jogging buddy spotted him and asked if he'd like to go backstage and meet the performers. The navy man introduced him to Miss Smith and a blonde starlet who'd caught his eye in the show and "a tall, brunet male star who was dignified and self-assured." West was shaking hands with Ronald Reagan. Handling the introduction was Ensign Gerald Ford. (Most Pre-Flighters were in Chapel Hill only three months, then off to flight training. Had Miss Smith's show come to town sixteen days earlier, the audience might have included Cadet George H.W. Bush.)

The Number of Deferments Asked Is None

The day after the Pearl Harbor invasion, Graham called what the *Daily Tar Heel* reported as an emergency meeting of students, planned "barely 30 minutes in advance." He asked some 2,000 students in attendance "to stick to their books and equip themselves in body and mind for any task they may be called upon to perform for their country." The newspaper went on: "His statement that 'we stand for free discussion and accurate information even in time of war' was greeted with a wild outburst of cheering."

That September the *Tar Heel* welcomed newcomers: "To any of the freshmen who are frittering under the misapprehension that Carolina is a playground, who plan to dawdle away a few pleasant months here before the draft board snatches them, we baldly say, 'Get out.'"

Graham had been a member of President Roosevelt's War Labor Board for eight months when Pearl was invaded. Meanwhile the civil libertarian in him never yielded. He coaxed the Labor Board to abolish the terms *colored laborer* and *white laborer.* Incensed at the internment of Japanese Americans, he fought the university trustees and faculty to admit a Japanese student and finally brought her in over their objections.

University departments as diverse as music, pharmacy, journalism, math, and philosophy, in recommending individual students for war service, were proud to add that they had requested no deferments. Others even used the war as an excuse to renew requests for programs and equipment they'd been denied before. Many would get new programs, though not, perhaps, what they had in mind. The School of Public Health studied malaria. Courses were begun in Japanese and Russian languages and culture. The chemistry department got expensive materials analysis equipment to study manufacturing processes. The Institute of Government had civilian defense officials lined up to test protective masks in its gas chamber.

In November 1942 Dean of Students Francis Bradshaw got a new job as dean of the College of War Training. Besides engineering the shift from liberal arts to the "arts of war," the new school had charge of creative changes in the academic calendar—and the admission of students who had barely gotten used to high school. At the height of the war, one could enroll at any of five different times during the year; this was tailored to shortened academic terms designed to speed up education before military induction and to offer quick classroom flings during furloughs. The university worked with high schools to enable many bright young people to skip the eleventh and twelfth grades and get in some college ahead of the draft board. Admission tests and personal recommendations were the only prerequisites.

By mid-1942 those ordered to Chapel Hill by the military began taking their places beside civilians. These students had extra incentive to work hard: A success went on to an officer's commission; an academic failure might board his ship as a mere seaman.

A Game Now and Then

The Pre-Flight School's newspaper kept referring to him as Theodore Williams. In Boston they knew him as Ted. He was the headliner of an all-star sports show, courtesy of the navy training programs, that livened the war years in Chapel Hill.

Cadet Williams hit a homer his first time up at old Emerson Field. He and Red Sox teammate Johnny Pesky and pitcher Johnny Sain of the Boston Braves made the Pre-Flight Cloudbusters one of the most feared baseball teams anywhere. One photo of the Cloudbusters showed twelve Major Leaguers. They needed the talent — on a given day they might face a Greensboro team with Pee Wee Reese or a Norfolk nine featuring Dom DiMaggio and Phil Rizzuto.

Williams had a special relationship with the dining hall. He dropped baseballs on the roof. In batting practice he hit the side of Lenoir on request. Legend has it, he hit 'em through windows and into 80-gallon soup pots, and the prisoners of war who worked in the kitchen would have to throw that batch out.

Lieutenant James Crowley, former Fordham University football coach and one of Notre Dame's famed Four Horsemen, coached the football team. In fall 1944 young Lieutenant Paul "Bear" Bryant was a Cloudbusters assistant coach. Doc Blanchard was the offensive star of a freshman team that almost went undefeated; he previewed the running that would power the famous army teams. In 1944 Otto Graham had the kind of season that got him chosen for the Associated Press all-service team.

One afternoon that same autumn, local fans got a glimpse of a kid just out of high school who helped Bainbridge Naval Training Center beat the Cloudbusters. He played only ten minutes. He got in a 65-yard bootleg for a touchdown. Charlie Justice had played his first game in Kenan Stadium, *against* Carolina.

Business Was Booming

The Depression had not been kind to Carrboro and its cotton mills. It was separated from Chapel Hill by some countryside then and was home to half the area's population. The war brought something for Carrboro, too. In 1942 the National Munitions Corporation moved into the abandoned

Durham Hosiery Mills Building 7, behind the Main Street shops across from Carr Mill Mall. Local people got almost all the 150 initial jobs.

The product was 20mm anti-aircraft shells, equal to twelve sticks of dynamite, and bazooka shells. Men packed shells with the high-grade explosive tetryl. Women applied the detonators. The work was messy—tetryl turned the skin yellow; nurses continually applied gauze to the blistered hands of those handling the shells. Once, it was deadly. Just before dawn on September 9, 1942, many people in the area awoke to what they immediately assumed was an enemy attack. It was the munitions plant; one man was dead and seven injured in an explosion in a mixing house.

The plant hummed for three shifts a day for most of three years. Its workers could fill 400 to 500 cases per shift, three boxcars at least twice a week. They earned three Army-Navy "E" citations for war production excellence.

Boogie Woogie Bugle Boys

One month before the explosion at the munitions plant knocked Rebecca Clark out of her bed, the band came to town. Already the navy had sweetened the pot at the university laundry where Clark worked for $9 a week. Uniform shirts had to be done just right, and as incentive, they were piecework—9 cents per, and Clark could make $25 some weeks. Now, band uniforms to boot. Better still, she said, "All of a sudden all the boys in my neighborhood wanted to be musicians."

Musicians who were racially barred from Carolina were recruited from Negro colleges, primarily the present-day N.C. A&T in Greensboro and N.C. Central in Durham. They went to Norfolk for six weeks of basic training. In August 1942 the forty men of the Pre-Flight Band arrived in a town for which they became as much a source of pride as any aspect of the military presence. "The kids would follow us around," said Walter Carlson, who had just finished college and been recommended to the band by his teacher at A&T. "We participated in events in the black community, and we taught some of them how to play. But what I really remember is how the kids would follow us around town."

The band settled into a routine of playing every morning during cadets' drills. The players were versatile—they might do a morning march, a full dress review at Kenan in the afternoon, then become an evening dance band at the Carolina Inn.

The members got honorary degrees from the U.S. Navy School of Music.

Rebecca Clark, who died in 2009, was an influential community activist. Her sons, Doug and John, grew up noticing that people were making money by making music for college students. They went on to make the Hot Nuts a name band all over the South.

Victory Village

Chapel Hillians remember navy pilots who returned to the scene of their cadet training by buzzing Franklin Street in their planes. Gerald Ford cut it a little close—he was involved in two crashes, one as a pilot, at Horace Williams Airport.

On campus the YMCA maintained a big board with regular postings of the chronicles of Carolina's heroes—the medal winners in North Africa, the missing in action at Midway. On Franklin, the Varsity did the same for Chapel Hill, its front windows papered with local people in uniform.

Those who came home acted as if they were still on a mission. The mood of the university underwent a noticeable change beginning in 1945. The wanderlust of the typical college student didn't make it back to town. Fred Flagler recalled a day in Bingham Hall when a marine veteran challenged a professor whose lecture seemed to be contradicting the textbook. The prof's flip response was not received well. "The marine said, 'I tell you what—you better find out what we're supposed to say on the exam, or we're going to hang you out the window,'" Flagler said. "I wouldn't have had the courage to do that. But they just weren't taking any crap."

The university's new challenge was finding places for everybody. The campus was crowded with Quonset huts and wooden barracks-style temporary buildings to house the overflow. The Tin Can, the old gym where often it was too cold to play basketball, was outfitted as a barracks-style dorm.

Married veterans have special memories of a place called Victory Village, a military-style encampment located in what is now the medical campus. Square, pre-fabricated, four-room buildings were brought from Camp Forest, Tennessee. Bill Friday, president emeritus of the University of North Carolina system, lived there after he returned from the war. "We had been through an amazing war experience, and we were profoundly grateful to be home," he recalled.

The Pre-Flight School closed in September 1945. The navy didn't take everything with them. When it weighed anchor, the campus had an annex to Woollen Gym, a new outdoor pool, and the football practice field, Navy Field. Seven decades of Carolina classes have used facilities built by or for the military: Jackson Hall; the Naval Armory; Nash and Miller halls (since razed); the original infirmary, now part of UNC hospitals; a major expansion of the airport; and the Scuttlebutt (also razed), whose privileges were limited to military people until after the war.

The navy-built facilities were valued at more than $1 million, and cost the university and state about $126,000. On the town side, Orange County sales tax revenues grew 31 percent in 1940–41 and 58 percent between 1940–41 and 1943–44.

Did the navy's presence keep the university from closing its doors during the war? Quite possibly. Civilian enrollment fluctuated during the war years between half and less than half of pre-1941 enrollment of 4,000. The law school, which averaged about 120 students in the pre-war years, dropped to nine civilians in 1943-44; the medical school had five students that year. But the military kept the enrollment at or above the pre-war level. And it gave the home front—town and gown—an exceptional sense of purpose in the war effort.

DAVID BROWN has been an associate editor of the *Carolina Alumni Review* for fifteen years. Prior to that he was a newspaper reporter and freelance writer, and worked in corporate public relations in North Carolina.

Standing Up by Sitting Down

CHARLES L. THOMPSON

I SPENT NEW YEAR'S EVE 1963 in jail in Chapel Hill. About half a dozen other guys, black and white and mostly young, occupied the four-person cell with me. But it was far less crowded than it had been during most of the sit-in campaign that fall. To keep our spirits up, we sang "I Shall Not Be Moved," "Wade in the Water," and other anthems of the civil rights movement. The women in the cell beyond ours sang too. We could not see them, but they sounded like angels. They could sing in harmony, and they knew how to let one high voice drift above the others for short solos, then come back in on the chorus. The concrete walls echoed lightly with their singing. They always saved "We Shall Overcome" for last.

I was beginning to think that this was one of my best New Year's Eves ever. I loved listening to the women sing, and there were enough guys to camouflage my own off-key efforts. Our main strengths were volume and enthusiasm. The women encouraged us with applause. They were generous as well as brave. At about 9:30, the mood changed suddenly. The police brought in several of our friends who had just sat in at a store called Carlton's Rock Pile on the edge of town. It was not a restaurant but a gas station and country store that stocked canned goods and Slim Jims and MoonPies. When our friends tried to buy a few items, the eponymous Carlton Mize told them that he did not serve niggers. So they sat down on the floor.

At most places where we sat in, the owners would get angry and shout at us to get out. But then they would just call the police, who would come and haul us away for trespassing. Mr. Mize did not do that. Instead, he locked the front and back doors. Then he brought out bottles of Clorox and ammonia. He poured them over the protesters' heads. When they gasped for air, streams of ammonia and bleach ran into their mouths. All of us who went out on sit-ins vowed not to offer more than passive resistance. So they neither moved nor fought Mize but shut their eyes tight and twisted back and forth, trying to keep the chemicals out of their eyes and mouths.

When we went out for a sit-in, none of us knew where we were going. But the leaders, including John Dunne and Quinton Baker, who were about my age, did know. A few minutes before the sit-in party arrived at the target, the leaders would notify the police. That call saved our friends from worse injury that night at the Rock Pile. The police arrived, peered in through the glass front door, and saw what was happening. They pounded on the door, but Mr. Mize ignored them and went about his business. Finally, either he relented or the police broke in.

The police took the demonstrators to the hospital to have their stomachs pumped and their burns treated. Some were then brought to the jail with little paper cups of thick yellow ointment. Each cup had a wide, flat tongue depressor to scoop out the ointment. As the demonstrators told us about what had happened, we put ointment on the worst burned areas. My friend James Foushee, a local black fellow whom we revered, put ointment on a white demonstrator sitting on the floor in front of him. I smoothed it on the back of a fellow I didn't know well but had seen in jail several times. It was the first time I had ever touched a black person's skin that intimately. I was careful; the skin on his back had darkened where the burns were worst.

To my shame, I was relieved that I had not happened to go out on the night of the sit-in at Carlton's Rock Pile. Shame was actually an emotion that I was very familiar with at that time, though I could not have named it. In fact, it was shame that had led me to get involved in the sit-ins.

What happened was this. A girl I knew had been one of the first to sit in. Karen Parker came from a well-to-do, well-educated family in Winston-Salem and was the first black person I had even known from a background similar to my own. We were both at the university, and one day I heard that she had been arrested after she had tried to get service in a restaurant. I was furious and astonished. Why anyone would lock Karen up for trying to eat in a restaurant was beyond me.

Yet on second thought, I asked myself how I could be either angry or astonished. I had grown up in the segregated South. Everything was segregated—not just restaurants, but schools, water fountains, bathrooms, theaters, buses, beaches, libraries, churches—everything. That was the way things were in my native Greensboro and throughout the South. My parents would have whipped us good if we had ever called anyone a disparaging name. But none of us questioned the established order. When the sit-ins at Woolworth's occurred, we didn't know what to make of them. When I saw pictures in the paper of white people taunting the young men from N.C. A&T and dumping Cokes over their heads, I felt embarrassed, both for the demonstrators and the taunters. It just wasn't dignified. But I had been part of this system all my life and had never raised a voice against it.

Karen's arrest changed that. I was deeply ashamed. I went to a meeting in Carrboro, on the second floor of a little brick building near Bill's Chicken Box. The meeting room was hot and crowded, and things were a little confused at first. Several people spoke, including John Dunne and Quinton Baker. I knew John through a friend from Greensboro who, like John, had won a Morehead Scholarship and pledged Pi Kappa Alpha. I had actually met John briefly when we came to Chapel Hill as Morehead

172

finalists, but I lost out in that competition. When we were in Chapel Hill for the finals, the Morehead people had taught us to sing "Ol' Black Joe" for the judges after dinner. When John spoke that night in Carrboro, the irony of our Morehead performance did not strike me immediately.

At the end of the meeting, the leaders asked all those who wanted to sit in that night to come forward. Few did. This made me angry, and I jumped up and walked to the front. John and others explained the ground rules. If attacked verbally or physically, we were not to resist in any active way. A couple of guys taught us how to protect ourselves passively, by locking our fingers behind our necks and curling up in a fetal position. We also got a lesson in going limp and staying that way during and after the arrest. More may have been said, but I was very frightened and had started to shake, I hoped not visibly. John or Quinton then told us the drill: We would not know where we were going until we arrived, and neither would anyone else but the leaders themselves. They would call the police before we arrived at the target for the sit-in.

I don't remember much about getting into the car, who was with me, or who drove. The trip, like my decision to sit in, was a contest between shame and fear in which shame won out. Two indicators will tell you how frightened I was, the first stereotypical and the second more subtle. The first is that my knees literally knocked together like a cartoon character. The second is that I had been voted "Most Courteous" in my high school class of about 500 students. To be the most courteous guy in a Southern high school at that time required a degree of regard for the opinions of others that can only be characterized as acutely pathological. So I had to be pretty ashamed of my complicity in segregation to overcome both real fear and thorough social conditioning.

My first sit-in was at the Pines Restaurant on Raleigh Road. We arrived, went in, and sat down without incident. There were seven of us, a mix of black and white, men and women, adults and college students. There were only a few customers, who stared at us but said nothing and kept their seats. The owner, in a firm but not rude voice, asked us to leave. We stayed put. Soon the police came. When they tried to remove us, we went limp. Two policemen hauled each of us out. I am 6-feet–5-inches and even then weighed about 210 pounds. So they half-carried, half-dragged me to a cruiser.

Lights flashing, the cruisers drove up to the jail, and the police pulled us out, not more roughly than necessary. I came to have great respect for the Chapel Hill police, or most of them. The police carried us downstairs to the small cell. Later, Chief William Blake complained to John and Quinton that his men were injuring their backs carrying us downstairs, and we agreed to walk this portion of the trip.

Each cell had four hard bunks, although after a big sit-in there might be twenty-five of us in a cell. After we settled in, we started the responsive singing that marked every night in jail. To this day, I can remember most of the songs. I think I was about as happy when we were singing as I have been in my life.

While we sang downstairs in the Chapel Hill jail, the university and the police were calling my parents in Greensboro. By "the university," I mean some representative of the university unknown to me, then or now. That person told my mother that I had been arrested for trespassing as part of a sit-in. My mother was shocked, of course. I had changed since I went down to what my father, an N.C. State guy, called "Whisky Hill." I wore my hair long for those times (though it was scarcely over the collar), and I affected blue turtlenecks under my Oxford shirts, along with jeans, which had replaced my khakis. I also wore heavy work boots instead of the obligatory Bass Weejuns. This getup made me feel a little awkward at times, but some of my more interesting Greensboro friends found it very daring, which pleased me enormously. The deconditioning of my conventional inhibitions had begun, even if it was off to a shaky start.

But other than these signs and the offbeat company I sometimes brought home, my parents had no warning of my arrest. It never occurred to me to warn them. My parents never chastised me for what I had done, nor reproached me for the repercussions they had to endure at work, in church, in the neighborhood, and among their friends. I learned about that only later.

After the call from the university, my mother called the police to ask if I was all right and whether I had a pillow and blanket. The police had the good grace not to announce my mother's call to my fellow inmates, nor to ask whether I was comfortable. In fact, I had no pillow, but we did have four blankets, one per bunk, and we shared them by lying on the floor side by side, alternating heads and feet.

The night of my first arrest we got nothing to eat, either at the Pines or in jail. But the next morning, I was introduced to jail food. Both breakfast and supper consisted of what we called *chilleh dawgs,* not ironically but simply because that was how we talked. Though there was always an admixture of Yankees, some from Duke, most of the folks in jail, black and white, were Southerners. This came to be a vexing identity for me and— I would bet—for many of my colleagues in the movement. We identified deeply with the South at the same time that we reviled and challenged one of its defining institutions.

The jail menu omitted luncheon. But I remember the pleasure of evening deliveries from Bill's Chicken Box No. 1, which featured fried chicken, barbecue, and hush puppies. A taste for this fare was one of the few things all Southerners, black and white, shared equally. It was wonderful. And it was free. I do not know whether Bill himself tore up the tab or it was paid by one of the white Chapel Hill establishmentarians who were said to support us discreetly. None of them came to visit us in jail. Nor did they identify themselves. They were rather quiet supporters.

In fact, we never got any sign that anyone approved of what we were doing except for the courageous endorsement by *Daily Tar Heel* editors, Gary Blanchard and David Ethridge. Their editorial was clear and deeply welcomed. They said we were acting for truth and justice and those who spoke against us were hypocritical gradualists or worse.

I participated in two more sit-ins. One was at Brady's, not far from Carlton's Rock Pile. Lots of Carolina students were eating there when we sat down at the counter. They glowered at us. Mr. Brady grew very exercised but only called the police. When they arrived, Mr. Brady growled, "Lock 'em up!" The next day there was a picture in the *Chapel Hill Weekly* of my girlfriend, Jo Johnston, being dragged out by one arm.

The other time I sat in was at the Tar Heel Sandwich Shop. Actually, we didn't quite make it into the shop, which was diagonally across from the jail. The customers inside saw us coming and quickly locked the door. So we sat down in front of it.

Someone opened the door behind us and started kicking the guy next to me, a young black kid from Mississippi. When he had been introduced to me as a volunteer for the Student Nonviolent Coordinating Committee (SNCC) just before the sit-in, I noticed his deep blue-black skin and brilliant smile. I couldn't see him during the kicking episode because I was staring straight ahead as we had been trained to do. The police soon came, and the kicking stopped. The police put us in cars for the half-block trip to jail.

As we were walking downstairs to the cell, the SNCC kid collapsed behind me. The police took him to the hospital. All they could do for him there was to tape up his ribs, some of which were cracked. When the police brought him back to the cell, he told me what had happened, and I cursed the guys who had kicked him. He looked at me silently, with a look that said, *You really don't quite get this, do you?* Then he smiled and shook his head. "They're just scared," he explained. We talked for a while longer, and I learned that he was sixteen years old and came from Greenville, Mississippi. He traveled throughout the South for SNCC, demonstrating and sitting in. If things were as bad as they were in Chapel Hill, I thought, how dangerous must it be to sit in in Mississippi and Alabama? Like the other volunteers I met, he combined an insouciant, off-handed courage with an almost saintly forbearance. And wisdom. At age sixteen.

During one of my stints in jail, another rough episode occurred. A sit-in group arrived at the Watts Motel restaurant on 15-501. There were more protesters than chairs. So Lou Calhoun sat on the floor and encouraged others to do the same. One customer dragged Lou toward the door. While he was lying there, a waitress stood over him and urinated on him. The customers applauded.

In jail I heard about other episodes. James Foushee told us about his experience at the Colonial Drugstore on Franklin Street. He sat down at the counter, and the owner, John Carswell, shouted at him to get out. James remained seated. Carswell went behind the counter, brought out a double-barreled shotgun, and leveled it at James's face. Cocking one hammer, he said he would kill James if he did not leave. "I reckon you are just going to have to kill me, then," James replied. Carswell called the police. The incident inspired one of our standard choruses for "We Shall Not Be Moved": "Tell John Carswell, we shall not be moved." James could not be moved. Like a tree planted by the water.

I met a number of courageous people during that time—the SNCC kid from Mississippi, Lou Calhoun, James Foushee, and several young black women who were still in high school. I thought a lot about courage and decided I was not courageous. To say that I *thought* is not quite right. I obsessed and agonized. After the Rock Pile incident, I pictured myself there and asked myself what I would have done. I felt that I was being cowardly, but I could not bring myself to participate in another sit-in. I marched and picketed, but I did not sit in.

I still think about courage. I now think that a person who does something that he believes in despite being afraid is courageous. Even if he does it out of shame. But what of a person who stops doing what he believes in because living with the constant fear becomes too difficult? Does he then slip back across the line from courage to cowardice?

During the months we sat in and demonstrated, we accomplished nothing locally. Not a single restaurant desegregated. Nor a country store. No supermarket began hiring blacks. No support for desegregation arose from the town or university. Except for the *Daily Tar Heel* editors, almost no one signaled support. Some local liberals even accused us of doing the town and university a disservice by moving too fast. People were not ready for desegregation.

In the summer of 1964, I was driving back to North Carolina from New Jersey when I heard on the car radio that the Civil Rights Act of 1964 had been passed. I had to pull off the turnpike for a while. Since then, I have come to see that our efforts in Chapel Hill did make a contribution. Just not locally. They were part of a broader pattern of flare-ups across the South. When the flames died out in one locality, they would flare up in another. Ultimately, the pressure was sufficient—together with JFK's martyrdom and LBJ's mastery of Congress—to prompt passage of the Civil Rights Act.

On the day the Civil Rights Act went into effect later that summer, I was with two friends in a Charleston restaurant overlooking Fort Sumter. Among the racially mixed crowd of fellow diners, a handsomely dressed white man surveyed the room. "What a difference a day makes," he said. I promise that this actually happened.

CHARLES THOMPSON graduated from the University of North Carolina at Chapel Hill in 1965. He left North Carolina in 1967, then wandered in the Northern wilderness until 1998, when he came home to Chapel Hill. He is Lora Wilson King Distinguished Professor of Education at East Carolina University.

I Raised My Hand

KAREN L. PARKER

IT WAS DURING A PANEL DISCUSSION at the opening of Wilson Library's exhibit, "I Raised My Hand to Volunteer: Student Protest in 1960s Chapel Hill." Even though it was now 2007, that evening shook me to the core.

I was on the panel because decades earlier I had participated in Chapel Hill's civil rights movement of 1963–64. The moderator opened with a reading from a UNC student's diary, dated June 23, 1964. The student, relating a conversation with her mother, spoke of her frustrations in trying to make a positive contribution to the world and wondering where she "belonged in the scheme of things."

It was my diary. I had forgotten about that entry and was surprised at the quality of the writing for someone fresh out of UNC's School of Journalism.

When I graduated in May 1965, I became the first black female undergraduate to finish Carolina.

The panel discussion unleashed memories of those years before the 1964 Civil Rights Act had passed—nearly all of them unpleasant and which

I'd long ago suppressed. As questions were directed at me, I found myself unusually tongue-tied. I was shaken, totally off my game, giving lame answers.

A few weeks later, I went back to the library to view the first part of the three-part exhibit about the civil rights days. I read lyrics of some of the "freedom songs," based on Negro spirituals, that inspired us just before going out to demonstrate. They brought to mind lines from some of my favorites:

> Oh freedom,
> Oh freedom,
> Oh freedom over me
> And before I'll be a slave, I'll be buried in my grave
> And go home to my lord and be free
>
> This may be the last time, this may be the last time
> This may be the last time
> May be the last time, children I don't know
>
> Ain't gonna let nobody turn me 'round, turn me 'round, turn me 'round,
> Ain't gonna let nobody turn me 'round
>
> Keep on walking, keep on talking
> Marching up to freedom land
>
> The only thing that we did wrong was let segregation stay so long
> The only thing that we did right was when we began to fight
>
> Keep your eyes on the prize, hold on
> Keep your eyes on the prize, hold on

And, of course, "We Shall Overcome."

Exhibited near the song lyrics were two letters warning that Negroes, as we were called then, should not have access to the same public facilities as whites, and urging Chapel Hill restaurants to hold their ground against our attempts to bring about desegregation. The words were vitriolic as well as racist. One letter attributed the civil rights effort to outside agitators — that usually meant Yankees and communists. How many times had I heard a white person state with certainty that "Our nigras were happy until these outside agitators came in and stirred them up."

Another letter opined that desegregation would result in black men raping white women.

The juxtaposition of something so malicious and something so uplifting felt like a slap in the face. I felt tears well up, and my emotions from long ago were triggered: How dare these people say that I am a lesser human being than they! I quickly left the room so that I wouldn't be seen bawling in the library. The hurt and anger that the letters provoked befuddled me. How could events of some forty-plus years ago so profoundly affect a self-proclaimed tough cookie?

Details of that desegregation effort have been well chronicled in John Ehle's *The Free Men,* articles in the March/April 2006 issue of *Carolina Alumni Review,* and in my diary, now on file at Wilson Library.

When I arrived at Carolina in September 1963, it was like a dream come true. I had seen parts of the campus previously and found it beautiful. Now I was there!

After orientation, I had a free afternoon to take in my new environment. I ended up on Franklin Street. It was one of those sunny, crisp fall days, and I was ebullient. I soon encountered the "flower ladies," who were a fixture on Franklin Street back in those days. The ladies were local black women who sold flowers from their own gardens. I bought a colorful bunch of fall flowers and a vase, and happily tripped back to my dorm to put them in my room. All seemed well with the world.

Three months later I would find myself in Chapel Hill's jail along with Rosemary Ezra, another student, and James Foushee, who lived in town. We had volunteered to go to a restaurant in Carrboro to attempt to get served. We knew what would happen—service would be denied and the cops would arrest us. Our instructions were to adhere to *passive resistance*, the nonviolent tactic advocated by Dr. Martin Luther King Jr.: When the police arrived, we were to drop limp to the ground and become dead weight, forcing them to carry us to the patrol car and into the jail. Our long-term goal was to fill the jail with demonstrators in an effort to force the area to abandon segregation.

Because Chapel Hill was fairly liberal compared to the rest of the segregated South, it was considered a good prospect for desegregation. Already two restaurants—the Carolina Coffee Shop, which is still in business on Franklin Street, and Harry's Grill, which was next to the old post office— had welcomed blacks on their own.

The movement attracted a mix of people—white and black Carolina students and a couple of faculty members; Chapel Hill blacks, primarily high school students; and students from N.C. College in Durham (now N.C. Central University). We were later joined by about a hundred white residents of Chapel Hill.

Although black churches served as formal meeting places, our informal gathering spot was Harry's. Oddly, some of the big persons on Carolina's campus, who would never have gone public, joined us in Harry's in a show of support.

The movement entailed marches, a hunger strike on the post office lawn, attempts to be served at white restaurants that resulted in arrest and jail, and a massive sit-in after a UNC–Wake Forest basketball game on a Saturday in February 1964 that blocked every major intersection around Chapel Hill. But each time we went out to protest, we weren't told about our mission until we got to the scene because someone had infiltrated the group and was tipping off the police, who sometimes got to our targets before we did.

The day we blocked the intersections, we were told only that what we were about to do might be life-threatening. This gave people the option of dropping out. Most of the group stayed. And, as I was sitting on the asphalt at Columbia and Franklin, I realized the danger as we blocked the path of the angry basketball crowd trying to leave town at the end of the game. I was relieved when the police hauled us away to the safety of jail.

As the movement picked up momentum, the ranks of demonstrators and arrests grew. Among them were a handful of white girls from my dorm, including my roommate, Joanne Johnston. In fact, Jo, who was from New Jersey but for the previous nine years had lived in Winston-Salem and Greensboro, logged more jail time than I did. A photo of a police officer dragging Jo along the ground from a protest at a restaurant became one of the most memorable of those times. Other dorm friends weren't into getting arrested, but they participated in marches and handed out leaflets.

The focus of the movement soon shifted to the many court cases— scores of protesters had been arrested. The movement seemed to fizzle out.

Desegregation of Chapel Hill's public places did occur—not because of our efforts but due to the passage of the Civil Rights Act.

In the spring, when I graduated from Chapel Hill, I felt depressed and bitter, frustrated at the difficulty in trying to effect positive change: Most folks seemed not to care. I had intended to skip graduation ceremonies—they seemed superficial and meaningless to me, but my parents insisted that I participate. After all, they had footed the bill for my education. So I reluctantly showed up at Kenan Stadium in a gown and cap.

As I was to write in my diary, I'd had that conversation with my mother about my depression and the seeming futility of our efforts. I was also in the job market and though I was sending out résumés, I'd yet to get a job offer besides the Winston-Salem paper, where I had worked while still in school. Besides, I was determined to leave the South and get away from all the ugliness of Jim Crow.

That July, I accepted a job as a copy editor and feature writer in Grand Rapids, Michigan. I soon got a surprise regarding racial attitudes in the North. On the surface, all was fine; but Grand Rapids had long-running discriminatory practices against blacks. This was the difference between *de jure* segregation in the South and *de facto* segregation in the North—the former being legally supported and the latter being unsupported by law.

Thinking back on my long-ago experiences at UNC and Chapel Hill, I have decided to put those angry, hurtful feelings that arose during the panel discussion and the library exhibit back into that jar of suppression and tighten the lid. They will never go away, but reliving them won't help any either.

When people ask me about my time at Carolina, the civil rights demonstrations and unpleasant encounters on campus are not the memories that spring to mind. I instead recall the many experiences that expanded my thinking and the dorm mates I got to know who are close friends to this day. But chiefly, I got a great education that has served me well in life and is fundamental to what I have become.

184

KAREN L. PARKER is a newspaper copy editor who recently retired from the *Winston-Salem Journal*. Since her graduation from the University of North Carolina's School of Journalism in 1965, she has worked for several newspapers, including the *Los Angeles Times*.

Life upon Life

(a poem to be read aloud)

WILL McINERNEY of Sacrificial Poets

I love the warmth of a wood-fire stove
heat blanketed on skin thick like the history of my home
you can feel it in the air, each breath
is a story
and as I sit in its presence, chapters of this book drip from my forehead
into a puddle of memories
waiting to be evaporated back into existence
I have become a part of its legend,
sewn in its spine.

My umbilical cord is buried in its eastern shadow
a native tradition affirming the connection of the people with land
we are one and the same.

I wonder
when it rains does the wood remember what life tasted like?
When you uproot a tree
is it like ripping an umbilical cord out of mother
is that why we've learned to cut them both
are we afraid of getting blood on our hands?

I don't believe in ghosts, only dead trees
what is my home but their cemetery
every board in the floor howls in the language of a forced relationship
dead tree skin takes blows from worn-out human souls
their rings are like brass knuckles trying to grind splinters of revenge in our heels
and their screams are battle cries,
bark muffled in sawdust bleeding from their gums.

I imagine every plank in this deck of a home
was cut from a tree that fell when no one was around
that's why they make so much sound now.

Believe me,
I've been to Jerusalem and back
stood at the crossroads of the crucifixion
and I can tell you there are holier trees in the floorboard of my home
that creak the gospels of Orange County
as my mother turns their pages with her footsteps
I memorized every verse,
that's how much faith I have in this foundation.

My home is like my religion,
filled with everything I love in this world
and a hoard of skeletons we don't like to talk about

There is a barn in the back corner of the yard,
with a door that's heavy on my soul
like the cover of my bible it's hard to open sometimes.
I can hear blasphemy in the hinges of its spine and
it cracks open like fresh welts in the Carolina heat.

I'm sure the wood that lines its walls still has nightmares,
nicotine soaked into the rings
like the space on my grandfather's fingers where he held cigarettes for 50 years
you can still smell the concoction of blood and tobacco soaking in fear
like Tar Heel confederate soldiers amputating their humanity in the rafters.

It is an icon of the past,
where they hung their harvest to dry and undoubtedly slaves to die
I'm sure the history of this house is haunted in the sins of the South
the clay is a little redder down there,
and the large oak beside it has grown higher in defiance
trying to keep its branches out of the reach of racists
whose closed minds found themselves on the short side of Chapel Hill's history.

Thought they were the judges of who takes life in order to live
as greed bled from their shallow calluses,
I imagine the scratch in her skin
that made their graves was a celebration for the earth.

My home
is riddled with rotting wood and new foundations for this world
I
am riddled in a rotten ancestry and high hopes for humanity
we have haunted histories, big hearts, and blood-soaked roots.

I swear,
sometimes I can still hear the boards whisper,
reminding me of the people who died before me
of the people who killed before me
that life is built upon life
that unforgivable sacrifices were made in my name
that I must be a guardian of life while I'm here

The boards remind me that life will be built upon me
that for better or worse
one day I too
will be a tree.

WILL MCINERNEY is associate director of Sacrificial Poets. An acclaimed spoken word artist, he placed first in the South and third in the nation with the Bull City Slam Team in 2010. He has taught poetry workshops for high schools in Chapel Hill and Ramallah in the Palestinian West Bank.

Views in Fiction 🦋

Rising Tide

ELIZABETH SPENCER

WHEN WILLARD COLLINS finally left that day, Margery didn't even watch him walk away. If she had done, she thought, closing the door, she would see going away with him all those types he had worked with, whom they had met at dinners, at cocktail parties, at the club, at the golf course. And their wives, too. The ones who worked were interesting but tired; the ones who didn't work were silly. She had liked them all, or had said she did. Those bankers, insurance men, presidents of this and that, doctors . . . all that bunch who ran things. But now they were walking away with Willard. She wasn't sorry.

Margery went back in the kitchen and poured some orange juice.

She didn't doubt he would come back for something, the house argument, money questions. Divorce was wearying business but over at last, so why for the first time did she feel unsteady, a sort of wobbling on her feet now that her thoughts were at their steadiest? And when, in addition, she had just received assurance of the *job*.

Oh that job! Margery thought. It was going to channel her thoughts and efforts. Business composition, even if she couldn't get a freshman English slot, would lead to concentrating on something besides breaking up with Willard. She closed her eyes and put out a hand to touch something, something stable and reassuring. She opened them and was okay. She took up the letter of acceptance and read it again. She had said that to her daughter Elise: "I've got a fresh start!" For as a friend had told her, "We're halfway through the Seventies, honey. It's high time for a fresh start."

Before she knew it, she was in it. She was entering a classroom full of waiting students, introducing herself, discussing, presenting, assigning papers. She came home weary but the weariness was a new kind.

A student named Sabra Blaine always sat in the same place, midway back on the third row, to her right. Margery Collins had judged him from the first to be from some Eastern country. Maybe he was from India, some obscure, oddly named place, inland on that distant continent. He was much older than college age. He was small, slight, with a head all but bald, just a fringe of hair left to circle the back. He was always smiling. Smiling to encourage her, was the impression she got. No matter what she said there was the smile. When she said anything halfway funny, he nodded with enthusiasm. He got it, he understood.

Arranging for student conferences, she wondered especially when his would be.

As it happened, he signed up for the final one at four-thirty, at the end of the day. So in addition to going over his critique of an assigned essay, she walked out together with him after shelving books, collecting papers, and locking the office door behind her.

He had agreed with everything she said. "Yes, yes, too sketchy. Yes, not accurate. Yes, I should look up." There was the accent, singsong, as she knew there would be, though he had never spoken up in class.

As they passed down the hallway and waited for the elevator, she ventured to ask if he was a foreign student.

"Foreign? Oh, yes!" he smiled with enthusiasm, as though the fact itself was a treasure.

"From where?"

He spoke the town's obscure name—*Champore* was how it sounded. "But many years ago," he added.

"Many years ago that you left?"

"Yes, left." They were passing the campus grill. He turned off from the path toward the grill door. "Please." He touched her arm. "I offer coffee."

For a moment she hesitated. Wariness with students had to be observed, and recently divorced as she was, she constantly felt she was learning new rules. But he was hardly the type to concern her, she thought and agreed.

Inside at a table, he assembled everything as though they were about to feast. Two coffees, milk in tiny containers, paper packets of sugar, spoons, napkins. The grill was all but empty. "Please," he kept saying, as he offered items to her. "Please."

Not until they both were stirring their cups did he start to speak. "My mother was movie star," he said.

She all but laughed. "Movie star? In Champore?"

"Zampour. Yes. By accident. She was beautiful. Just a girl. They came there with a company to make movie. The director saw her carrying up water from the river. The movie was all around the river—crocodiles, cows, children, muddy places, all that is every day to Zampour. He asked about my mother. The next day he looked for her. He found her and asked her to come let him take her picture."

"Then . . . ?"

"Then he put her in movie. She was driving cows, two, down to drink from river. Also he fell in love with her."

"He married her?"

"Only for short time. To bring her to the States. Also so as to let her have me, as legitimate child. But citizen . . . American. Always he intended leaving her."

"That's a sad story," she murmured. "So you aren't a foreign student."

They were silent. He was sipping his coffee. His teeth, she noted, as she had before, were almost the color of coffee, as though he smoked a lot. Or didn't they chew betel nut — something she had heard.

"Sad story," he repeated finally, and smiled his usual smile, which she could not interpret. Its meaning kept expanding. Did he smile in acceptance that life was sad, or from some philosophic attitude? Had some religion led him into it? And why, if he had come here as a child, or even to hear him tell it, as an embryo, did he speak with such an accent?

As though he knew what she was thinking, he said, "My mother took sick after so few years here. She prepared everything before she died. She sent me back to India to live with grandparents. Grandparents took note of facts. I am American. So, they said, I can come to America."

Margery agreed.

"I must get education. Education is very necessary. Without it, no one would have job."

"It's true," she said.

"Now," he said. "You have husband, house, home? You have children?"

"I have a daughter in college. I'm divorced."

"That is sad story?" It was almost a question.

"I suppose so. At first I thought it was. Now, I think that maybe it's a — well maybe not happy — but a necessary story."

He waited.

But she told him no more and he began to smile again.

"I speak Hindi. Also dialect of Zampour. You wish to hear?" She didn't especially, but he said some strange phrases anyway.

Walking back to her car, she wondered at how quickly they had come to confiding. She had the feeling he was lonely. Had he no one here? No friends? Certainly no family, from what he said.

A week later she saw him on campus with a young girl taller than himself, wearing very short shorts and sandals. Her legs were long and thin. She was brown-skinned, and might possibly also be Indian, Margery thought. So he had found someone. But maybe she was a classmate, in some other class.

The day after this sighting, Sabra Blaine lingered after class and again accompanied her down the stairs.

"You will find someone soon," he told her. "You are blonde."

What's blonde got to do with it? she almost snapped, but did not. His assumption that she was looking for someone irritated her. Dr. Marino, the psychologist she sometimes saw, listened carefully.

"You feel vulnerable since you left your husband," he said. "He may be wrong, but do you have a reason to think he was insulting?"

"I suppose not." Still she was dissatisfied.

Afternoons, when Margery came home from the university, her daughter Elise was often there, either looking at TV or snacking out of the refrigerator. There was a thin wall of small quarrels between them, something apt to go on indefinitely; it often vanished altogether, only to return. Elise wanted to have a year of study abroad. Her father favored this but could not afford it. He could, he promised, help her mother afford it. Her mother didn't want her to go. She had other uses for the money. And was Elise grown up enough to look after herself? Her tumbled dorm room, her disorganized study habits would tell you no, but changes often took place when other scenes and people took over. Perhaps she would manage all right, in company, of course, with other students. The matter was still unresolved and meantime Elise complained. Food was her special subject. She liked Chinese food. "I can't cook that," Margery had told her. "I can't begin to learn. Buy it frozen. Or we can send out for it." So they did, at least once a week. Elise usually returned to the dorm, but last night rain had blown in on her bed because she had left the window open. "I didn't notice," she said. "I didn't even hear it. I'll sleep here tonight. It has to dry."

"Does she miss her father?" Dr. Marino asked.

"She never says so. She can go spend weekends with him whenever she wants. Lately she hasn't mentioned him."

"Girls her age are often restless," the doctor said. Was he Spanish or Italian?

When Sabra Blaine got into trouble he sent for Margery. She went down to the police station where he had been detained, to see about him. He had a cut on the side of his face which was still bleeding and his clothes looked dirty and scuffed, pulled about. They were about to take him up to the emergency room at the hospital to get him sewed up, but first she had to be told that he had gotten into a brawl at a fraternity house.

"You are related?" the officer asked in some wonderment, as nobody could look less kin to Sabra Blaine than she.

"Not at all," she said.

"She is friend," Sabra said. When he smiled, more blood came out. He was holding a towel to his face.

"At the fraternity house? They should have called the campus police."

"It didn't stop there," said the officer. "They kept it up downtown."

"Who did this?" she asked. "He must know who it was."

"He doesn't know the name or doesn't like to tell us."

"I would tell you," said Sabra, "except that in fraternity they thought I was stealing something. If I tell who hit me, he will say what he thought and I will have to prove it not true. This I do not wish. Now we go to hospital?"

"Do you vouch for him?" the officer asked Margery.

"He's a good student, an A student. I teach business composition and reading comprehension."

It was Saturday. Margery waited in the hospital waiting room while Sabra Blaine got sewed up, endured penicillin and tetanus injections, and was bandaged. They went out together.

"I must get lawyer," said Sabra.

She started. "Why?"

"Things broken up. A very hard fight. In a way, I like. How good to strike. But now to pay for everything. Lawyer, estimates, repairs...."

What had started at the fraternity house, it turned out, was that Sabra was searching for Paula. Paula was the thin, long-legged girl Margery had seen him with. She had gone to the fraternity house with a student older than she.

"You were jealous?"

"She is like sister, like little sister. I know she would find no good in that house. They hid her from me behind the curtain. But I knew. I seized curtain. It all came down. Crash on a table. Many things broken. She was there. I was right. 'Paula,' I said. 'You must leave now.' Then he struck me."

"Did she leave?"

"She did. I tell you, she is like sister. She knows when I speak like family speech."

"So what next?"

"This student followed me to town. He came out of alley. I was about to eat in a restaurant. Bar-B-Q. We fought. There was police and he ran. If I would say his name, they would find him. I do not wish to say."

"You mustn't get yourself in trouble now," she warned him. "Any more of this and the university—"

He raised his hand. "No more! I promise!" Then he laughed as if everything had been a joke, a sort of playing bad instead of being so.

"Sabra, do you have any money?"

"Money?" He looked at her oddly, as if he didn't know what that was. He looked as if he might pay bills in elephant tusks and crocodile skins. "Come. I buy you coffee."

Instead she drove him home. Home was a dormitory room, the very end of an old building, just at the edge of a sharp slant in the terrain and looking as if it might slide off. "I have coffee," he offered. "Tea also."

Margery shook her head but inquired: "Sabra, why did you choose me to help you? You've got other teachers, don't you?"

He considered carefully. "You have face of understanding," he concluded. "That is good."

Maybe I have, she thought, driving away. *The face of understanding.*

Margery wondered why she had troubled about him. Then she grew busy with other matters and forgot.

Sometimes she went to see her grandmother, old Mrs. Tenny, in her apartment at the retirement home. Mrs. Tenny, in her nineties, had outlived all her children. There were ways, Margery thought, that extreme age was helpful, even endearing. For example, Gran knew better but felt they were all of them present. Just where, she wasn't sure, but certainly around somewhere. She frequently mentioned them.

She sat in an adjustable reclining chair so as to watch TV without propping up. Margery sat near her and held her hand. Mrs. Tenny switched off the screen. "Lilla," she began, "didn't bring cakes this week." Margery's Aunt Lilla had been dead at least ten years. Yet cakes did appear at times. Someone remembered to be thoughtful. Mrs. Tenny had a large connection, some alive, some dead.

"I should have brought some," Margery said.

"Store cookies," said Mrs. Tenny, though without criticism. "Still, she sent that gardener." She nodded toward the window and at that moment a lawn mower began to purr.

Though it was only a small lawn in the complex of condos, Mrs. Tenny fretted over the grass and nagged the staff until she got plants put in. "Please, Margery. Go tell him to weed the impatiens," she said.

Margery went from the room to the side door, which opened on the little lawn. There right before her was indeed the lawn mower and driving it was Sabra Blaine. She cried out his name in astonishment. He looked up and stopped the motor.

"Oh, Miss!"

"What are you doing here?"

"I cut lawn. Is job," he added.

"I can see that," Margery marveled.

"Much good to work outside," he continued. "Fresh air."

She asked him to weed the impatiens.

"I know him," she told her grandmother. "He's my student."

Mrs. Tenny was scarcely impressed. "Wonders never cease," she remarked and went on to ask about Elise, her only great-granddaughter.

"Most of the time we get along," Margery said. "I think girls growing up are difficult, don't you?"

"You never were," Mrs. Tenny smiled, her little present for the day. "But Lilla told me Elise was going out with a black boy. Is she?"

Margery started. She knew that Elise dated at times but never pushed to inquire unless the boy turned up and she met him. She had once talked over the question with the Dr. Marino. It was better to leave her alone unless she wanted to talk about something.

"Not that I know of," she said.

"Well it's not for me to order the world," said Mrs. Tenny. "Maybe he's from Haiti."

"If he exists at all," said Margery.

"He could be nice," Mrs. Tenny said comfortably. "The olden ways are gone." Opening a box she found some cookies. "Lilla must have been here. I don't remember."

When Margery returned home she heard talking from the kitchen. So it was Elise with a boyfriend. She was divided between pleasure that the girl would bring a boy home to meet her and a little wonder if maybe what somebody had mentioned to Gran might be true. She went on resolutely and called out her daughter's name, entering. The two looked up.

"Mother," said Elise, "this is Carlos."

Okay then, Mexican. What did she know about them? Margery wondered. But what, she also added to herself, do we know about anybody? Certainly her husband's year-old affair with a colleague's wife had caught her off guard. It was the colleague who had exploded. No patching up after that, as he had immediately filed for divorce. Maybe I should have done that too, she often thought. Instead she let things play out, going from bad to worse until the competent, able sort she had married turned bored, inattentive, even abusive. A year of trying to improve things failed.

"I'm learning Spanish," said Elise.

"She is good," said Carlos. "Buena."

"Then you can teach me," said Margery. "Are you staying for dinner?"

He consented. At table he went on to tell all about himself.

Carlos had lived in a house with a dirt floor until he was ten. Then his mother got a job with an American family, in the town where the father worked for a car company. They made parts for cars cheaper than they could make them in the States. Soon the family got Carlos's father a job in the company and that made money coming two ways and meant a better house.

Carlos seemed not to think what had happened to him was remarkable.

"You had luck," Elise said.

"Everyone likes my mother. She is so loving. Not only to me. To everybody she is together with. Mexican people are not so loving. She is the different one. So—" he shrugged—"all life is changed."

"Because of your mother," Margery half inquired.

"It is strange, don't you think?"

"No," she said. "Not so strange. But I think the lady she worked for had something to do with your good luck."

"Oh, yes." For a moment he concentrated. "That lady was unhappy."

Elise and Margery were silent, waiting for him to explain. He ate for a time, pulling at his piece of chicken breast with his fork, pushing large hunks into his mouth. He had nice brown hands. The whole of him scarcely seemed anything but admirable. He noticed they were waiting.

"Her husband sent their children to school in the U.S. She wanted them there. There was an English school in Puebla, near to us. He wouldn't send them there. Soon I went to that school. I learned to speak. You can see. I was like adopted."

"Adopted by them?"

"Not really." He touched his breast. "In the heart."

"Do you see them?" Margery asked.

"No more. They got angry with my father. He got the workers together for more pay. He did not succeed. Then there was no more work, no profit. Everything broke down."

Margery had been to Mexico once with Willard. It was the summer before Elise was born. In fact, it was near Puebla, she now remembered, that she always believed she had conceived in a Best Western motel. She remembered the outlying roads, the poor shacks, children playing with live iguanas, holding them up to sight like baby dragons. Hoping to be thrown a few pesos or a U.S. quarter. The dry, rutted streets led eventually to a smooth modern highway and the motel sign. The air conditioner worked.

"But they were good to you," she burst out.

"Yes, very good," said Carlos and continued eating. Then he suddenly, looking at Elise, offered a whole explanation in Spanish. Elise said, "Oh, I see."

She followed her mother in the kitchen as they cleared off plates. "What did he say?" Margery asked her.

"I couldn't make it out very clear, but I think he said his father was a drunk. He hated Americans. But Carlos doesn't."

"Well that's good," Margery said, thinking of a nice family trying to help out some poor people they liked. They wanted them to "get ahead in life." Maybe to some people that didn't mean anything. First it was just a cause for resentment, then for rebelling. It made her angry to think about it.

Elise often changed boyfriends. When asked what happened to the previous one, she would say, "Oh, he's around."

"Didn't you like him?"

"Sure, I did. But not enough."

Enough for what? Margery worried, but thinking she knew already, she didn't ask.

At the retirement home, Sabra Blaine no longer mowed the lawn. A black man now pushed the mower. "They come and go," her grandmother said. "The black ones are best. They seem to like doing it." Then she began to laugh. "Oh, Margery," she exclaimed. "For some reason, I was thinking of the house party."

Margery knew what she meant. At the time it had been funny.

She was asleep down at the camp they rented each year for a sorority party. She was fuzzy from having had too much to drink the night before. Even knowing they weren't supposed to, they got liquor anyway, mixed up with some sort of punch, and drank and acted silly.

There were some boys coming later. A bunch was down by the lake. It was past twilight and getting dark when she fell asleep. She was startled awake with a black face leaning all the way across the bed, not an inch away from her own. She screamed. Not once but twice and maybe more. Then the boy got up and ripped the black mask off, an awful mask with thick red lips. He was laughing at her and of course she had to laugh too, though shaking still and almost in tears. "Jes call me Rastus," he said. She didn't even know him, though why that would have made any difference she couldn't say.

"Why on earth did you remember that?" she asked her grandmother. She had come home and told all about it. Her mother had sympathized ("The idea!" she said) but Gran had giggled.

"Just thought of it. I don't know why. I just lie here and think of things. You'd be surprised what things I think about."

Margery imagined that she would.

"For instance," she continued, "did I tell you that Willard came to see me?"

"What on earth for?" Margery asked.

"Well, he mainly just walked around and around, but he did tell me that you were dating a Chinaman and that Elise had got mixed up with some Indian."

"That's crazy. Just forget it. Promise."

"I promise."

"Have other job now," said Sabra Blaine. "Waiting tables at Mandy's Restaurant. Is cooler."

She was talking with him in her office about a paper he had submitted in which he set forth an argument that disturbed her. He proposed that when going into a business arrangement that if promising something did not suit the one who promised it, a complete denial of having promised it at all was not only permissible but might be used to advantage, that was to say, purposely.

"You realize," said Margery, "that this is not good business procedure. It would quickly get you a bad name."

Sabra nodded, smiling happily. "Must use carefully," he agreed. "Not too often."

"But I mean," said Margery, "it's wrong." He was silent. "Don't you think so?"

"Is useful," he murmured, almost to himself. "In business useful is good."

"Not if it's wrong!" She was aggrieved.

Carlos came to dinner again, bringing a large melon. Margery asked Elise later if she really liked him. "He's very sweet," Elise said.

That weekend, Willard showed up. He had called to inquire if he might come by. In the living room he walked around, talking. He had always been nervous and inclined to pace. "She tells me she has this Mexican guy," he threw out, as though Margery had caused something.

"Yes, I've met him," she said.

"What's he like? She even wants me to meet him."

"Well, wouldn't that be natural?"

"Getting parents involved. It sounds serious."

She sighed. She also had doubts. "I guess we have to be tolerant."

"I'd rather know who I'm being tolerant about. I mean to say that if we object she might take to defending him."

Margery well remembered that her family had disliked Willard and look what happened.

Willard went to the kitchen, opened the refrigerator, and drew out a beer. He returned with it, guzzling from the can.

Willard was not a bad-looking man. He was rangy but well built. He walked with a careless stride and seemed always on the lookout. He suspected life.

"She's had a good many boyfriends," said Margery. "Maybe this one will go along with the others."

"Maybe I'll say I'm busy," said Willard. He found the garbage and tossed in the empty can. "I'll say I'm out of town. Will call when I get back. Maybe by that time she'll have somebody else. Or maybe I'll see him. What do you think?"

She started to add something about the good name Carlos had given to his mother, but Willard would find that laughable. *So he likes his mother*, he would say. *Well well. . . .*

"I'm not holding off because of the boy," he continued. "He may be okay. It's only that pretty soon we'll have the whole family crowding around. I know the type. It's just as well not to monkey around with that sort. Talks about them, does he?"

"He likes his mother."

"So he likes his mother. Well, well. . . . Are they hooking up? You know . . . is he laying her?"

"I wouldn't think so. She stays in the dorm when she's not here."

"You'd better steer off that bunch, Margie. Get shut of him." Now it was his Southern small-town voice, which she had once liked so much until she had actually listened to what it was saying.

Still, he was good at business, and maybe she didn't have to take his ideas seriously. As for other women in his life, didn't some wives "look the other way." He sometimes called up at night, late enough to apologize (though he didn't), wanting her opinion on something. Had she been hasty? She wondered, but didn't know.

A week later a smiling, polite, overweight woman came up to her in the grocery store. Her face was round and pretty; her black hair was pulled straight back and fastened in a knot. She wore a loose cotton dress and sandals.

"So your daughter knows my son," she began.

Margery allowed that was so.

"My Carlos is first-class boy. You should know that."

"He's very polite," Margery admitted.

"They would make nice babies," the woman said.

"What an idea!" Margery exploded and walked off.

She stewed with anger the whole afternoon. What did she mean? Maybe that *if* they got married they *would* make nice babies? Or were they making nice babies *now*? Back to Dr. Marino? No, she wouldn't. She would talk to Elise.

"I haven't got time to make babies," Elise laughed. "I've got to graduate. I'm working real hard, Mom."

Margery agreed. "So don't get into real sex," she advised. Surely that was the right precaution.

"Oh come on," Elise said. "You know that Indian guy."

"Ridiculous," Margery said. "Where on earth did you get that?"

Elise giggled. "I think Carlos knows him. He talks about you."

Willard stopped her in the parking lot at the grocery. "Is Elise serious?"

"About what?" Margery asked.

"She says you are dating some guy from India."

"Of course not," Margery said. "He's just a student."

"Oh," said Willard and left.

The Indian guy worked hard in her course, heeding her admonitions about his business morals, though she suspected he did so only on paper, to please her.

"I do not have to work restaurant or mow lawns," he told her. "I receive money from my father the movie director."

"How was that?"

"I write to him, a most pitiful letter. I say I defend girl much abused, which costs money."

"Was that true?"

"It might have been," Sabra Blaine said blandly.

So what business was it of hers, she thought, where he got his money or how? Still, she was annoyed.

A week later, visiting with her grandmother, she came out with the latest. "Now they want to have a party!"

"Who wants to?"

"Carlos and Elise. They just want something like a cookout, but if it's still chilly, they think we can just fry up some burgers in the house."

"Oh well, why not let them? It won't kill you."

She finally agreed. Elise set the night. She made out a list of names, twelve in all, though it kept changing. Sabra was on it and Paula, Carlos, of course, and other names which mostly sounded everyday American.

"They're bringing everything," Elise warbled. "I said I'd buy some drinks."

Exam time was winding down. It was a time for summer plans and parties before leaving. Time, thought Margery that evening, for the doorbell to start ringing and so it did.

If there was any word to describe how the young guests came in, it would be "discreetly." They were quiet and polite, meeting Margery in her creamy slacks and blouse, saying hi to Elise and Carlos. Sabra wore a little cap. His tall friend had on a skirt. All were ready to loosen up as minutes passed, so that by the time they had carried their sacks into the kitchen and set to work, there were giggles and chatter coming in waves.

How they were organized! Did they do this all the time? Elise knew the whole routine, knives and forks, paper napkins, ice for Cokes, burger patties in the grill, buns and onions. A football-player-sized boy dumped salad in their biggest bowl. His tiny girlfriend poured on the dressing. A cry of "Mustard!" sounded like an operatic wail. In the living room, moving a chair, a pair of girls almost knocked down a row of blue vases, which teetered, but stabilized. Margery held her breath over the vases, then thought it was better to keep completely out of the way. She fled into her study and closed the door. She tried to concentrate on grading. She smelled frying meat.

When the door burst open it was Sabra, carrying a plate of hamburger, potato chips, salad. "Must eat," he instructed and went to fetch her a Coke.

She knew what Willard was probably thinking. *Of course, they'll all get drunk.*

Not true! she wanted to reply and was right. Out in the house, it grew quiet. They were feeding and so was she. But then the hum rose again, increasing; now Elise came in, wild-eyed. "You've got to come! Mother, you've got to come and see!"

So what now? She stood on the outskirts of the swarming living room. Cheerleaders, they told her. Two were "real," they said, and four more knew how. It was going to be a pyramid. A little red-haired girl in chopped-off jeans stood bravely, while two more each grabbed a leg and hoisted her to their shoulders. Three more lined up below, lifting the first three. Would the redhead bump the ceiling? Almost.

"Which were real?" Margery asked, but got no answer except from Elise who said, "Sabra knows one." Two were black, one white as milk. One, a limber black girl in the middle, had skin like polished jet. There were low chants that everybody knew, mounting, rising.

WIN WIN WIN!!! GO, HEELS, GO!!!

SCORE SCORE SCORE!!! DEE-FENCE, GET TOUGH!!!

GET TOUGH!!! DEE-FENCE!!!!

The red-headed girl lost balance. She swung side to side. Margery held her breath again. Broken bones were worse than broken vases. Shrieks all round. The red hair, tilting, was a flaming torch. Arms rose up to her, brown, black, and white. Hands caught her by the ankles and she steadied. Everyone clapped. A milk-chocolate-colored boy, off in the sidelines, sat calmly beating a little drum. Sabra Blaine squatted cross-legged in the corner, looking like a cross between Buddha and Mahatma Gandhi.

The pyramid came carefully to earth. Cheers. You'd think there really was a game being won. Margery was laughing at nothing, elated with everything. She felt excited and young.

How they cleaned up! Washing, scrubbing, bagging scraps and trash. How they thanked her! Elise hugged her; so did Carlos. "It was great . . . it was great . . . !"

Margery had not gone to bed so happy in such a long time.

The next day in her office at school, Willard called. Could they meet for coffee?

She was pleased, for she wanted to tell him about the party. They sat in a booth at the grill.

"No, Willard, nothing at all to drink. They were like cherubs. And such a mixture."

"I almost came," he surprised her by saying. "Elise told me."

"You could have," she returned. She felt a bit put out. It had been her good time.

"Was there a Mexican invasion?"

"Only one or two. No kin to Carlos," she added.

"What's that you got?" he asked.

"Latte."

"Funny they call it that."

"Why?"

"Just coffee and milk."

"It's Italian."

They sat silently. He stared at her. "So you brought it off?"

"I didn't do anything really. Elise did it all and the kids."

"Margie, I got the boundary fixed for you. They'd copied the survey wrong."

It was a tax error, he meant.

"Thanks," she said. "It saves me going over there."

"You wouldn't have known how," he pointed out.

She was sure they would have helped her.

"Then there was the car insurance. I got the adjustment through."

"Well, it was your accident, not mine."

"We needed to change the car title."

"Things do get mixed up."

He sat silently for a time, then reached to take her hand. "Wonder why we did it."

"Why we split, you mean? I thought it had to do with Janice and Bob."

"They split."

"I know."

"That's all past." He went thinking on, holding her hand.

"Is there somebody else?" she asked cautiously.

He shook his head, but she knew him well enough, the way he dropped her hand, to guess that probably there was, so when he said, "Of course not," she almost laughed. "Is she white?"

He must have been holding his car keys in his other hand, for he went white himself and banged the metal on the table, rising in a fury.

"See you around." He slammed the grill door behind him.

Back in the office, Sabra Blaine eventually came in, asking for his grade. An A made him content, but he noted her latent tears.

"Is unhappiness?" he inquired.

It was a relief to tell about Willard. "I was just joking. I didn't mean it. He always takes things wrong." She thought of the flame-haired girl, tilting atop the pyramid, and the multicolored arms from white to jet black, reaching up. She burst out, "And what did it matter anyway?"

Sabra meditated. "Is difficult. Some seek many years for endings, but never find. But you — you succeed!" He smiled at her.

Sabra was thinking of leaving for India and starting a business. He would deal in beautiful Indian things — scarves, shawls, rugs, much else. "You will buy," he told her and beamed her his blessings.

Endings, she thought with relief. *Sabra is right. I succeeded.* Perhaps she said it aloud, perhaps not. She felt he knew it anyway.

They left the office together. She kept on walking with him without knowing why. The past was dissolving behind her.

ELIZABETH SPENCER is the author of nine novels, seven short story collections, a play, and a memoir. Her books include the novels, *The Night Travellers, No Place for an Angel,* and *The Light in the Piazza,* which has been adapted to the screen and stage. She is the five-time recipient of the O. Henry Award for short fiction.

The Beautiful Couple, Everyone Says So

LAWRENCE NAUMOFF

LESLIE AND KAREN rent a one-room house in Chapel Hill. They are students. It's the Sixties. A lot is going on. Things are changing and also not changing. There are doctors, for instance, who won't give unmarried women the pill. There are insurance companies that won't cover maternity costs for unmarried women, and there are Florence Crittenton Homes, sometimes gloomy and Edwardian, where the girls, who couldn't get the pill, go "away on a vacation" or "to spend the year with relatives."

Karen has done an art installation about these homes, and these girls. It's made of cardboard and dolls and small dresses and shoes and little bonnets and painted faces. It's very scary to look at, though not as scary as being there.

She has not ever been to one, though, where she might have seen that the girls have their babies taken away from them right after the birth. She and Leslie know someone who went through that. It seemed awfully mean, to treat the girls that way, they tell each other.

So Leslie is married to Karen. It was his idea. She liked the idea. It's a good life. They're seniors and she's an art major. They are part of the literary/artsy set in Chapel Hill. Lots of undergrads are married. Some of the women hold out until marriage. Not many do. It makes them crazy when they do, and then they marry almost any man who seems not like their father.

Before she got with Leslie, Karen once had to fly to Puerto Rico, to terminate the ---. She doesn't like to mention the, you know. It's only natural to feel that way. That was in her sophomore year, when it happened.

At this moment, though, in their little house overlooking the woods, Leslie has undressed except for green suede shoes he bought in London. His hair is a pale, sun-bleached auburn and he has the body of the swimmer he was in high school. Karen looks like Faye Dunaway, and she looks that good without makeup and special lighting.

Their friend, Lila, comes in off the porch. They have a project due and are making a sculpture of Leslie. Lila will work on the back and Karen on the front. They are using plaster over a life-size papier-mâché form.

"Hi, Lah-lah," he says, using the name her new boyfriend has given her. None of her boyfriends let her keep her real name. Why do they always name me something else, she asks Leslie.

Karen brings him a long-stemmed pipe with a tiny bowl on the end. The bowl has flowers painted on it and is ceramic. She puts the match to it.

They live on Cobb Terrace, a circular dead end two blocks from the university, at the bottom of the hill below the Franklin Street post office. It's a house made from a 1940s era one-car garage, the kind that had a wooden floor, which, in fact, is now the floor of the house. It is perched on the edge of the road, so that the front door is on the same level as the road, but the back side is seven feet off the ground, on piers, because the land falls away so fast, down to a gorge and a stream in the woods. The house is hard to heat. There is no furnace except for an unvented Warm Morning gas heater that makes both of them feel lightheaded as if they've smoked something bad. They don't use it much, but it's on today. It's February.

Students and temporary bohemians live in the second-floor rooms that many of the buildings in the main block of Franklin Street have rented out. It's a shabby life, above the stores and restaurants, with the bathroom for most of the rooms, "down the hall." It's real, though, like Kerouac or Hubert Selby Jr.

In the Cobb Terrace house, smoke from the little bowl drifts toward the two girls and Karen refills it, and then they consult with each other and agree to do each side of him unrelated to whatever the other person has imagined to do on her own side.

"Very cool idea," Leslie says.

She has strung a rope swing, with a seat made from stretchers and canvas, off the joists of the attic scoot hole. It's not for kinky anything, it's a childhood kind of thing. For her. He leans on it, and now and then spins around from the boredom.

"Be still," Lila says.

She looks like Sally Field—not the Flying Nun—but the one in the movie where she's a prostitute, not that Lila looks like a prostitute, Leslie has said to his wife when they figured out who she reminded them of. She does have decidedly hard good looks, however, as if she's older than they are and has been in prison. She wears miniskirts so short that everything shows, even when she's standing. She dates bad men. It's just, she says, she doesn't know they're bad until it's too late. Leslie and Karen are so lucky, everyone knows this.

He is patient. He's a good sport. He's been painted before, just never sculpted. The three-dimensionality is curious. The tactile aspect of the girls working on his body is odd to him. When he tires of standing in the pose, he again swings back and forth in a lazy arc, his shoes scraping the floor. The floor is dirty. They have never swept it in the eight months they've lived there. They do not own a broom.

————————————

This is the best year of Leslie's life. He is a writer, and as he graduates, he wins the Discovery Award from the National Endowment for the Arts. Karen wins the senior prize for her diorama. They throw a party.

Lila and everyone else in their crowd come to their house and spill out into the woods for that end-of-the-year, going-away party, which lasts days. Leslie's grandfather has left him $35,000 and he pays for the party out of it. He and Karen love each other, and all the people there, and everyone is in love, in just the right way.

They cry at the party, and they cry a lot, thinking about going away and never seeing each other again and how everything will change. The crying feels so sad it's beautiful, it's like art, their lives have been art, they didn't even know it would be that way, but it happens, and the party goes on until everyone has to leave town.

With four phone calls they tell their parents goodbye. It's not important, as neither are close to their parents, who are all in second marriages. Leslie describes his father as basically a man colder than liquid nitrogen and existing in a state of permanent irritation. Unlike some of her girlfriends, Karen has not been fortunate enough to have a mother who is her pal for life. She doesn't tell her mother anything. Her mother is disappointed in her, so disappointed, in the early marriage, an "artist," all that stuff, same old stuff. This lack-of-parent thing makes Leslie and Karen closer. They talk about it. They understand each other.

They will pack up their van and head to Mexico. They will be expatriates, and live cheap, and will have their friends down to stay with them in the shared house on the Pacific Ocean near Mazatlán.

This has been the best year of Karen's life, as well as Leslie's, though there is a difference. Even though this is clearly the best year of her life, she is somewhere else in her mind, and he does not know this. She is trying not to go there, trying not to worry about their future, and about him. The idea that he has no idea about their future and isn't thinking or talking about it, other than being a writer, worries her.

But in that year, that last year of school, their lives are as much a piece of art as what they write and create, things that often contain remnants of childhood mixed up with show-offy decadence, all of it like play, like a giddy thrill ride.

But in that year she sees even more clearly that he does not understand what it means that she is not there, not really there. She is sometimes afraid of what she is thinking.

They are a beautiful couple, they are perfect together, their friends all say they are, and they are married and they are artists and they will be famous, their friends tell them this. All of this is true, but they do not know what they are. Leslie and Karen do not know what they are. They, themselves, know who they are, but they do not know what they are together.

This is what she sees. It is like the deep, hollow sound of a cello that she feels, always there. As if her insides are the hollow insides of the cello. As if the sound is what she feels and hears, all the time, but because no one else hears it, she does not say anything. And yet, it is true, in this last year of school in Chapel Hill, in their Cobb Terrace digs.

It's the year of so much, then, the year when Kemp's funky record shop—the last wooden building on Franklin—burns down in a gloriously horrible fire, which they watch, and later walk home with the smoke and ash in the air all around them, and Karen says, he had so many cats in there,

I wonder if they got out, and Leslie says, it was stunning, though, the color of the flames, and they are quiet for a moment, before they talk about it, and they decide, that in some way, even that was beautiful.

And so this, then, this will have been the best year of their lives, for a long time to come, it really will have been, but they do not know this.

LAWRENCE NAUMOFF is the author of seven novels, including *Taller Women, Rootie Kazootie,* and *A Southern Tragedy in Crimson and Yellow.* He is the recipient of the Whiting Award and a National Endowment for the Arts Discovery Award. He teaches Creative Writing at the University of North Carolina at Chapel Hill. This piece is the opening of a longer short story, with the same title.

The Library

(Selections from *Entering Ephesus*)

DAPHNE ATHAS

THE TOWN OF EPHESUS was called the oasis of the South. This was because of the university. The university vied with the University of Georgia in claiming to be the oldest state university in the nation. It had a liberal tradition. There were only three thousand students. Everybody knew everybody else. Tuition was cheap. Many students were poor. Learning was respected. Philosophy was on everybody's lips. It was a last outpost of Jeffersonian simplicity and Greek humanism, and it was respected throughout the state.

Stories were told about how many miles famous alumni had traveled by mule or walked barefoot to get their education. Spirit and tradition were contagious because of the perfumed leaves and lawns. The campus was centered around an old well, over which had been built a fresh white canopy with columns. Old North and Old South were dormitories that had been designated state landmarks and planted with plaques. Dogwood perforated spring like snow. Oftentimes classes were held outdoors.

Teachers came from the North and West and spread the school's fame. It took on a cosmopolitan air.

Ephesus had pride in its democratic ways. It was forced to defend itself each generation from accusations of being a hotbed of Communism. It put out plans for countering erosion, unemployment, and tenant farming. Its mystique was contagious. The Shakespeare authority of Ephesus had been a hog-farmer, who interspersed footnotes with hog lore. He had taken up Shakespeare, he said, so he would never have to leave Ephesus. Another man connected with the university had written a book about Ephesus called *The Magnolia Tree in Heaven* and afterward committed suicide. Ephesian wits said it was because he had no place better to go. Everyone knew that the F-sharp of the bell tower was flat, but people had heard it so much during supper hour at Swine Hall that the false scale had become real to them and they preferred it.

Juxtaposed with the Apollonian dignity of the town was an underside, frenzied, eccentric, and passionate. It existed because, as in all college towns, most of the inhabitants were young, and people were fervent in their ideas and tried to live them. In the Twenties a Middle Westerner named Herbert Boll had established the Folk Blood Movement. He got the college to build a true Dionysian outdoor theater out of native stone, and there he put on Euripides and Sophocles with choruses of drawling coeds dressed in cheesecloth costumes and followed by gnats. This was not popular. So he decided that the drama should be indigenous. A school of playwriting grew up under him which featured tobacco-spitting mountaineers, exploited Negroes, mill workers being persecuted by scabs, witches, mountain conjure women, and tenant farmers holding the state's red earth in their hands, like Scarlett O'Hara's father, poeticizing against painted backdrops of pine trees. The theater was acclaimed nationally, and drama conventions were held there. It happened one year that a student murdered his friend in a rooming house and then rushed to the Folk Blood Theater and shot himself. Soon after, people noticed that the stones of the theater were turning red. Although the color was from iron in the stone, not blood, the movement got its name from this. Afterward the theater became a focus for two more murders, a suicide, and a strike. But at Ephesus everyone accepted the bizarre as a natural part of life, and although people made the most of these episodes for gossip, wisecracks, and telling the year by, they acted urbane.

A one-track railroad brought coal in once a week for the university power plant. This railroad track separated Ephesus from its adjunct, a settlement called Haw, originally Saxapahaw, Indian for "Dirty Feet in Muddy River." Although Haw was the original settlement, a weaving mill had been put there in 1910. The mill had gone out of business during the Depression, and the low brick building sat like a ghost, in the middle of the town, its great windows broken and squinting. Twisted black machinery still sat inside the mill. Sometimes children sneaked in to explore. Otherwise its silence remained unbroken except for field rats that forayed in from the railroad tracks, skittling around the forgotten piles of lint, or swallows that made nests in stacks of defective BVDs.

Haw was a scattering of mill houses clumped along dirt roads. Each mill house teetered on four stones at the corners. There were no foundations. The dirty white clapboards were stained red on the bottom from clay. Yards were grown up with weeds, choking bushes, or kudzu vines that had multiplied dangerously. Paths had been worn through the yards by bare feet. These paths were more traveled than the roads. The tin roofs gave off a feverish luster on hot afternoons in summer when the sun began to go down. People sat on their broken porches. Through the groan of their swings they stared out of sharp faces, the color of turnips, and they chewed tobacco. Underneath the houses dogs howled in their dreams.

It was in its relation to Ephesus that Haw was peculiar. It was the pole of a dualistic universe, the servile, dirty, ignorant underdog to Ephesus. The Ephesians ignored it. They let it stand ugly in the sun. But the Haw people knew the lacy lawns of Ephesus, the magnolia-tipped excellence, the green aspirations of the university, the promise of its halls, the enticement of its books, the lushness of its arboretum, the

221

secret of its learnedness. And they had no part in it. Despised, out of work, they sat like living ghosts in the sun and watched when the professors rode by.

———

Urie was early. She stood in the dirt road, dressed in an unsuitable black velvet skirt. The sun, already high in the molten sky, refracted off the tin roof of Lucretia Pile's store. Inside the door hole, through the baggy broken screen, was darkness, exuding a dank smell compounded of sour sweat and earthen beans. Two passing colored women eyed her furtively.

"What she doing?"

"Look like she praying in the middle of the road."

They disappeared into the maw of the store. Inside, a melody of Negro voices began.

A half-eaten watermelon lay exposed and bled on an upturned barrel in front of the store. The dust in the road was pocked with shining black seeds, and flies buzzed and seated themselves on the rind. All around, the sun was brilliant and searing, pouring a scorching light on the hills in the distance, thrilling the railroad tracks into fire-ribbons, and settling the baked earth of the road so that Urie could feel the heat through her shoe soles.

Zebul came up the railroad tracks. When he saw her he began to run. He arrived out of breath.

The unspoken mystery of where she lived caused an embarrassing silence between them. He pointed to the railroad tracks.

"See those railroad tracks?"

"Yes."

"Railroad tracks are basic to American life. Remember them. They opened up the country. But they made the dividing point between people. They are the crux of everything. By your position in relation to railroad tracks you are crap or noncrap."

She sensed what he was up to, but she did not say anything.

"It was not more than a quarter of a mile from this spot that I stepped in the nigger's hand," he said confidingly. "Have you ever heard that old cliché, living on the wrong side of the tracks?"

"Sure."

"Well, here is the dividing line. Right here." He drew a line with the sole of his sneaker in the dust of the road where they crossed the tracks.

Suddenly Urie saw that he was right. She had never thought of it before. She opened her mouth, but she could not think what to say.

"Which side do you live on?" he asked.

"This side."

It was true, then!

"Well, you literally live on the wrong side of the tracks," he announced. He stared at her significantly.

Her long, straight, aristocratic nose and soft, wide-open mouth awed him. Her blue accusing eyes inspired him.

"I live in the middle of Niggertown," she answered him, lifting up her chin the way she did at school, and pronouncing her words in the careful, strange accent she used. "So that proves your point. But I come from a place different than this, where people are not prejudiced, so I don't care whether I live in Niggertown or not. Nothing can make me low, because I don't believe people are lower or higher unless they *act* it."

He was strangely moved.

"I am not prejudiced either," he whispered, squinting against the sun. . . . "I am different like you are different. Because I come from Haw. That must be why, without even knowing you lived in Niggertown, I told you about the nigger hand. Just from osmosis. I'm talking about what people think, not about what is! You understand what I mean? There is something fated about my meeting you and about my knowing you would be my friend. And here I don't even know you. Yet here we are in the world, and I understand everything about you, and you do me, even if we don't know anything!"

In the silence a dozen eyeballs, disembodied like black and white marbles, peeked out of Lucretia Pile's baggy screen door at them.

"The beginning of the route of triumph and success," he told her, "leads that way"—he pointed up Pergamus Avenue—"to Ephesus. Everything gets better and better. The houses get bigger. They don't have tin roofs. They have real shingles. The road to degradation, ignorance, and stinkingness lies that way—to Haw. The houses get crappier and crappier. The roads turn into dirt. All the roofs are tin. And there are many chinaberry trees."

"Which is worse? Niggertown or Haw?"

"Haw."

There was a long silence.

"Where do you want to go first?" he asked. "Ephesus or Haw?"

"Ephesus," she said.

The first sight on the route was the power plant. As they passed it, they inspected it. He talked about it, describing it with adjectives. It was a giant, cannibalistic power plant with its tall, dithyrambic brick chimney which sucked, ate, chewed, and spewed out smoke from the coke which the weekly freight train brought in.

Next to the power plant was the university laundry. It had a water-refining tank behind it. Little jets of water spurted up into the sunlight, causing rainbows.

"There are the fountains of Versailles," said Urie.

They walked down Pergamus Avenue until they came to the Ephesus Inn. They entered the campus. It lay manicured and fresh as a newly cut sandwich, its tea-party lawns sliced by red brick gutters and paths. On the campus they became hushed and inspired.

They went to the Old Well. It was a colonnaded oval where a shining bubbler spurted a winking jet of water. It had been the first well of the university in 1858. They took a drink out of it.

A bell rang. Students came out of yellow brick buildings and sauntered to their next classes. Zebul and Urie followed the students to the book exchange. Students hurried to and fro, buying Coca-Colas and notebooks. One student bought an ice-cream cone and licked it. Zebul and Urie turned around and went out. Urie remembered the ice cream P.Q. had bought the first night they came to Ephesus. She pushed the ice-cream cone out of her head.

"Do you wish you had money?" asked Zebul.

"Yes," said Urie. . . .

They walked down the main campus toward the library. The chime in the bell tower rang eleven o'clock.

"I am going to college here," confided Zebul.

"You are?"

"Yes."

"How will you pay tuition?"

"Maybe I'll get a scholarship."

"Does it cost much?"

"About seventy-five dollars a term. And there are two terms in a year. If I don't get a scholarship, I'll get a self-help job."

"You can get jobs?"

"Sure. They have this thing called NYA, like WPA, which makes jobs so indigent people can go through college. Maybe I will work in the library."

Below lay the library, eight Greek columns with Doric capitals, great graceful glass doors like reflective eyes.

"The library is the focal point of the university," he said.

They walked step by step toward it. It was the shape of the Parthenon. The smell that came out the swinging doors toward them was cool, bookish, and echoey.

"Let's go in!" he whispered.

"Are we supposed to?"

"Of course!" Actually he did not know whether they were allowed or not, but because she questioned, he bade, his authority staked on it.

Step by step they mounted the stairs. They stopped under the columns, looking upward.

"Isn't it beautiful?" he asked, reveling.

She walked away from him to a column and knocked upon it as if to say "Open, Sesame."

"What are you doing?" he asked.

"Knocking the column."

"Why?"

"To see if it is fake."

He was shocked. "What do you mean, fake?"

"Haven't you ever tried the columns of the Baptist church?" she asked.

"No."

"They are all fake. They are made of tin cans."

He thought it was marvelous that she should know facts like this. They walked through the portico, knocking on each column.

"They're real. They're all real!" he said in triumph.

"Yes."

"Let's go in now."

They entered through the glass doors. Once in the elegant foyer, they were awed by the tallness of the high green dome, the marble floor, the chiseled staircase, the cold draft, and the whispers. They clung near each other, inching toward the carved banisters that led to the second floor, the Main Library.

"Are you a bookworm?" she whispered.

"Yes."

"I am too."

There was a naked statue of a Woman of Learning with nothing on and a book in her hand. She stood at the bottom of the stairway near a glass display case showing pictures of textile machinery.

"I am going to this university too," Urie suddenly announced.

Her words felt momentous. These were the first words since [her family] had arrived in Ephesus that gave a definite direction to her future. Yet the minute she had spoken them, it seemed settled and lost all importance.

On the way upstairs they passed a drinking fountain. They bent down and drank out of it.

"This is the fifteenth fountain we have drunk out of on this campus," said Zebul.

"On this campus they don't have any fountains for niggers," said Urie.

"That's because there aren't any."

"Do you know what my sister did in Richmond, Virginia?" Urie asked. "She almost drank out of a Negro fountain because it said 'Colored.' She thought it was pink water!" She poked Zebul, and suddenly he began to laugh. They laughed feverishly all the way up the stairs. Then they clapped their mouths, looked away from each other, then controlled themselves, gulping and blinking until they were worn out.

At the top of the stairs there was another statue. It was of a naked boy faun taking a splinter out of his foot. He had a wicked look on his face, and his big toe pointed to the card catalogue.

"Urie," said Zebul.

"What?"

"Let's take out a book!"

"Can we?"

"Sure."

"But what if it's just for college students?"

"All they can say is No, isn't it? We'll say we are students. They'll never know whether college or high school."

"How old are you?" she asked.

"Thirteen, but my birthday is in sixty-four days."

"I am one month older than you," she said.

"Be very nonchalant," ordered Zebul.

He headed for the card catalogue. She followed him. He opened a drawer. It was like a mouth opening. They stared at the names, thousands of them slipping before them.

"I'd even work typing commas on these cards," whispered Urie, "if it would pay for my tuition."

He closed the catalogue. *Ponk,* it sounded.

"Sh-sh-sh," she warned.

He opened another drawer, "*Tad* to *Try.*" He moved the cards. He came to TOLSTOY, COUNT L. There were hundreds of cards under Tolstoy. He chose one: *My Confession.* He wrote the number on a slip of paper.

The attendant behind the check-out desk, a fat student with pimples and green skin, looked over at them.

"Come on. It's your turn now," whispered Zebul.

She moved to the catalogue and flipped past Tolstoy. Her eyes caught on: "*To the Lighthouse,* V. Woolf, auth." She took the slip that Zebul handed her and wrote down the name and the number. Her heart was beating. She peeked over to see if the fat attendant was still looking at them. He wasn't.

Clutching their slips, they moved to the big oaken desk. Behind was an opening into the stacks, filled with book trolleys and stacks for cards. The fat student was gone. A huge clock above the desk stared down at them, its fingers pointing: eleven-fourteen. A man with warts came to receive their slips. Urie's toes curled inside her shoes. Zebul stared at the clock, pretending boredom. They waited while the man disappeared into the stacks. They did not look at each other. After what seemed an interminable time, the man with warts reappeared. They still did not look at each other.

As the man with warts lifted a stamper to stamp the slips he asked, "Are you students?"

"Yes," said Zebul.

He banged the stamp on the slips and then on the books. Urie's eyes were riveted to the spot, just next to her name and her address, which she had written illegibly in case there was a question. Then the man handed over the two books. Urie's was a dark, small wine-red edition. Zebul's was a green so dark as to be almost black, frayed at the corners, with a plastic binding out of which threads protruded.

"Don't run," warned Zebul. Clutching the books, they passed through the huge reference room. Miles of shelves. Miles of encyclopedias. A thousand long tables with lights perched like Florida birds. Outside huge vaulted windows were the banner-blue sky and the leaves of archaic trees whirling brilliantly like batons. They passed the faun, the Woman of Learning, ran down the stairs, by the glass cases of textile pictures. They pushed their way out the glass doors, ran through the columns, and catapulted down the stairs two at a time. Suddenly they were free on the sporty green campus, their books in their hands. They laughed in triumph.

DAPHNE ATHAS is the author of a number of books, including award-winning novels, *Entering Ephesus* and *Cora*. Her book, *Chapel Hill in Plain Sight: Notes from the Other Side of the Tracks,* was published by Eno Publishers. She taught Creative Writing at University of North Carolina at Chapel Hill for more than forty years.

In the Rearview Mirror

A Love Letter

Written upon the Occasion of My Departure

NIC BROWN

Dear Chapel Hill,

ONCE AGAIN, blood keeps getting sucked out of my balding forehead and carried in minute mosquito torsos through the humid air of my malarial neighborhood. In the floodplain behind the Rainbow Soccer fields near an OWASA water treatment plant, my neighbors and I run to our cars, swatting. The interminable wait between placing my daughter into her car seat, buckling her in, and closing the door produces welts across all uncovered flesh. But someone just wrote to me that mosquitoes barely exist in the dry elevation of northern Colorado. And this was music to my ears. Because in August, I'm leaving you and moving there. It's not you, it's me. I'm leaving for a job. And if I can keep your mosquitoes on my mind, it'll make things much easier. Because in sixteen years, you've laid claim to more than just my blood. An obsession with the bloodsuckers might just keep me from lingering on the rest.

In 1994 I buzzed my Volkswagen east from Greensboro and into your city limits for the first time. I was seventeen. I played drums with my band at the Skylight Exchange, then slept on a couch on Mallette Street. Behind closed doors slept girls who had graduated high school with my older brother. I awoke woozy on the thrill of college detritus around me and ambled a few inches off the ground toward Franklin Street, looking for my car, but was stopped by the sight of a pickup truck filled with elves. A marching band filed past. Shriners threw candy at me. It was Christmastime and I was stunned by this civic celebration. The effect was enhanced by the same emotional math that ensures a favorite song will sound better on the radio simply because it surprises you. The blue station wagon, the fire truck, Boy Scouts in line; it was like discovering a cheerleading competition in your front yard when you take out the trash. I'd been imprinted by Franklin Street. You were, from hence forth, magical and odd.

A year later I visited again and slept in the back of my friend's Dodge Dart. Fifty miles from Greensboro, I felt like I was adrift on a wide sea of culture and cool, dozing in that seaworthy Dodge. I couldn't have felt more romantic, more dangerous and alive.

You were my Manhattan. My Los Angeles. It seemed like there was nowhere more culturally explosive. Everyone was jaded. People were smart. They didn't wave when I drove past. The bands were terrifyingly hip. I fell in love.

I moved here when I was nineteen. I met my wife in a house on Short Street when she entered the living room as I tried to fit my torso through an unstrung tennis racquet. The weirdness was heady and profound. I slept late in those days but would sometimes awake early to friends climbing in my window.

We moved. To New York, then Iowa. But we always came back, mentally and physically. My wife is a Chapel Hill native. It was like marrying into royalty and returning to the hereditary homestead. And now: Our daughter was born here. I've become what I always wanted—a part of you. A townie.

So, Chapel Hill. Your Carolina mosquitoes can keep my blood. I'm telling myself it's a down payment on our future. I can come up with more. That stuff is like love—a surprisingly renewable resource. It just keeps generating itself from itself. And I'll need an immaculate multiplication, because along with my hemoglobin, I'm leaving a good portion of love with you and I don't want it back. Keep it. It's yours. It'll float around on whining wings, swatted at by people I used to see every day. But they won't be able to kill it.

Yours,

Nic Brown

NIC BROWN is the author of two novels, *Floodmarkers* and *Doubles*. He has been a columnist for the *Chapel Hill News* and for several years was director of communications at the Ackland Art Museum. A North Carolina native, Brown is now a professor at the University of Northern Colorado.

About the Cover

The cover illustration for 27 *Views of Chapel Hill* is the work of Chapel Hill writer and artist Daniel Wallace, who also wrote this book's introduction. His illustrations have appeared in many publications, including the *Los Angeles Times*, *Italian Vanity Fair*, and *Our State Magazine*. He also illustrated the book cover of 27 *Views of Hillsborough*, published by Eno Publishers.

Award-winning Books from Eno Publishers

27 Views of Hillsborough
A Southern Town in Prose & Poetry
INTRODUCTION BY MICHAEL MALONE
$15.95/216 pages
Gold IPPY Book Award, Best Anthology
Gold Eric Hoffer Book Award, Culture

Chapel Hill in Plain Sight
Notes from the Other Side of the Tracks
DAPHNE ATHAS
FOREWORD BY WILL BLYTHE
$16.95/246 pages
Finalist, Eric Hoffer Book Award

Undaunted Heart
The True Story of a Southern Belle & a Yankee General
SUZY BARILE
$16.95/238 pages
Silver IPPY Book Award, Best Regional Nonfiction

Brook Trout & the Writing Life
The Intermingling of Fishing & Writing in a Novelist's Life
CRAIG NOVA
FOREWORD BY ANN BEATTIE
$15.95/152 pages

Rain Gardening in the South
Ecologically Designed Gardens for Drought,
Deluge & Everything in Between
HELEN KRAUS & ANNE SPAFFORD
$19.95 /144 pages
Gold Book Award, Garden Writers Association
Silver Book Award, Garden Writers Association
Silver Benjamin Franklin Book Award
Honorable Mention, Eric Hoffer Book Award

Eno's books are available at your local bookshop and from www.enopublishers.org